A Message from Beyond

Suddenly to my amazement, letters I had not typed began appearing one by one on the computer's blank screen, as if an unseen hand were pressing the keys. FIND MY KILLER!

Something hard rattled against the windowpane and I jumped, my teeth chattering. It was as if my twin's personality had been dismembered and strewn over her room, and the cold wind teasing the back of my neck threatened to gather her pieces and return Isabel to life.

I heard laughter, and the back of my neck prickled. The silvery, high laugh sounded again, then died away into the sound of the wind.

TWIN SISTERS

JANICE HARRELL

SCHOLASTIC INC.

New York Toronto London Auckland Sydney
Mexico City New Delhi Hong Kong Buenos Aires

ISBN 0-439-71510-5

Copyright © 1995 by Janice Harrell. Cover illustration copyright © 1995 by Jim Carroll. All rights reserved. Published by Scholastic Inc. SCHOLASTIC, TROLL, and associated logos and designs are trademarks and/or registered trademarks of Scholastic Inc.

12 11 10 9 8 7 6 5 4 3 2 1   4 5 6 7 8 9/0

Printed in the U.S.A.   01

First Scholastic printing, November 2004

CHAPTER 1

I took over my sister's life after she died, slipped into her place without missing a beat. I wore her favorite fuzzy sweater, kissed her boyfriend, and inherited her friends and her enemies. It hadn't occurred to me that her killer would try again. Because of that oversight, I nearly ended up dead myself.

For Isabel the end came one hot day in late August, but for me that day was the beginning. To be more exact, everything began six days later, when I got the news of her death. I was sitting on the balcony, soaking up the warm Roman night and envying the Italian kids below me, who were climbing off their motorcycles, hiking up tight jeans, and streaming in pairs into the disco next door to our hotel. The roar of motorcycles drowned out the music that poured from the open door of the disco. The air was heavy with exhaust fumes.

Rome was busy and glamorous. I loved it, but we were only passing through. It seemed we were always passing through. What I wished for was a permanent address; a place where I fit in. I didn't know it, but I was about to get my wish—which shows that you should be careful what you wish for. What I was conscious of at the time was only that I was fed up with my life, sick of going from chalet to cottage to hotel with Mother, while other kids my age slept in the same bed every night and grew up with one set of friends.

It looked as if Mother was going to marry Simon Blandsford soon and move into his big house in Sussex, but I figured that when she finally put down roots it would be too late for me. I felt like a human suitcase with a lot of tired destination stickers plastered on it and frayed luggage tags trailing from the handles. "In transit" is a state of mind, like sadness, and I was beginning to think that for me it might be permanent. I had spent summers in Maine with my Hilliard grandparents and had gone to school in England, without having the slightest sense that I belonged in either place. When the weather turned foul in England, Mom had a way of heading off to Switzerland for skiing, or to Rome or the Bahamas to find the sun, taking me with her. In my mother's view, schoolwork was optional and friends could be replaced. All I knew was that no place felt like home. "Resident alien" might as well have been tattooed on my heart.

I stepped back into the drawing room. Mother hung up the phone and turned toward me with an odd look on her face. "That was Grandfather Herrick . . . calling from the States. Isabel is dead."

"No!" I cried. "She can't be dead. He's got it wrong." Mother didn't know it, but I had a letter from Isabel hidden in my suitcase. It was full of underlining and exclamation points; she was excited about our plan to get together next year, when we'd be away at college. She couldn't be dead!

Mother twirled the emerald ring on her thin finger. Unlike me, she was tiny—fragile and blond, with a faded prettiness that still drew men to her. "It seems incredible," she went on. "So sudden— it's hard to take it in. I'm afraid your father isn't in very good shape either. He had a heart attack when he found her. Your Grandfather Herrick has been trying to reach us for days. He finally got our

London address from the lawyers, but it took him a while to catch up with us."

My knees seemed to give way, and I sat down suddenly in the hotel's flowered armchair. The unbelievable—that Isabel was dead—was beginning to sink in. "What happened?" I asked.

Mother paced with quick, nervous steps, the heels of her delicate Italian shoes clacking briskly against the marble floor. "She must have surprised some intruder. Richard had left her alone while he went to Richmond for a few days to work in the library. I don't have to tell you that any beach cottage Richard chose would be perfectly isolated. Your father prefers sand dunes to people. Obviously she was killed while a burglar was robbing the place—Isabel's car and purse were stolen. Your father only has himself to blame." Mother nervously lit a cigarette and sucked on it until its tip glowed. "When he came back late one afternoon, the front door was open and Isabel was lying on the floor, dead. The shotgun blast had destroyed her face." Mother shuddered. "Horrible. Your grandfather said flies were buzzing around her head. Richard managed to dial 911, but then he went into shock, naturally."

For a second the strange sensation that it was

my own body lying lifeless on the floor overcame me. A painful sense of longing and hopelessness gripped me.

Mother stared out the window, her eyes filling up with tears. "My poor little baby. Who could ever dream something like this would happen? I thought we'd have time to get to know each other someday. And now she's been blown out like a candle. Gone."

I glanced at my mother in surprise. If she had any thoughts of getting together with Isabel, she had kept them quiet. Every time I mentioned going to see my twin, it threw her into a panic. That was why I had kept it a secret that Isabel and I had been writing letters back and forth for the past year.

"I'm going to the funeral," I said.

Mother wiped her eyes and blew her nose. "Don't be ridiculous. You can't do that."

"I don't think it's ridiculous to go to my own sister's funeral."

"You didn't even know her, Liz."

I smiled bitterly. "Next best thing, though—I practically *am* her."

Mother flicked her ash into a saucer. "Don't be morbid!" she snapped. That was unfair, since it was Mother who had told me time and again that Isabel and I, identical twins, were virtually the same person. We had come from one egg that had split in two. That was why when our parents divorced their novel approach to the custody question had struck them as so clever. Dad took Isabel and Mother took me. Since we were carbon copies, they figured the division was perfectly fair. It wasn't fair to Isabel and me, of course, but we were only three years old at the time and nobody asked us.

I had always wondered why Mother hadn't insisted on keeping both of us. Surely no court would have given custody of a three-year-old girl to a man as eccentric as our father. If only Mother had put up a fight for Isabel! But my theory was that she regarded Isabel as the "extra" baby. Mother had expected only one; twins had been a shock. When she left Isabel with Dad, I think she was actually relieved. She certainly didn't seem conscious of any loss.

For me it was different. I always felt as if part of me were missing. When I was small I dreamed of my twin constantly. I remember begging to go see her, but Mother had been surprisingly firm about refusing. Finally I caught on that the last thing she wanted was a lot of visiting back and forth. That would have meant having to deal with my father. She was determined to close that chapter of her life and be rid of him for good.

Now that I was practically grown, Mother couldn't stop me from going to Sewell's Falls to visit Isabel if I wanted. I wouldn't even have to get the money for the plane fare from her because I got an allowance from the trust fund Grandma Hilliard had set up for me. A few months ago at breakfast, I had told Mother I was thinking of going for a visit. "What makes you so sure you'd be welcome at your father's house?" she had said, buttering her toast. I had heard enough about how strange my father was for that to make me hesitate. In the end I had done nothing. I bitterly regretted it now that it was too late. Isabel was dead.

"Where is the funeral going to be?" I asked. "They haven't already had it, have they?"

Mother made an impatient gesture. "There isn't going to be a funeral. You know how strange your father is."

Of course I knew. If Mother hadn't told me a thousand times, I could have found it out easily enough by looking him up in the *Reader's Guide to Periodical Literature*. My father was Richard

Herrick, reclusive author of *Time the Magician,* which was required reading in high school literature classes. He had written other books that sold well, but none that brought in the mega royalties of that one. *Time the Magician* was the story of a teenager who faces a crisis of conscience and stands firmly on his principles. To me it seemed dated. I can't even remember the last time I heard somebody say the word "conscience." Of course, my schooling had been pretty spotty. It was very possible I wasn't capable of appreciating great literature.

"Richard plans to have her body cremated," Mother went on, "as soon as the police release it. There are certain . . . formalities in cases like this. Your Grandfather Herrick suggested there might be a memorial service once your father is out of the hospital, but in my opinion that's wishful thinking. Your grandfather keeps clinging to the illusion that Richard is a normal person." She shook her head. "Of course, Richard would rather die than do anything to call attention to himself. A memorial service—*hah!* Our wedding was so quiet you would have thought we were fugitives from justice." She stubbed out her cigarette. "This is a man who has his groceries delivered so he doesn't have to go out to the store. I remember when he tried to have his driver's license picture taken with his sunglasses on!"

She had launched into her familiar list of complaints about my father almost as if she had forgotten about Isabel.

"I'm going anyway," I said, interrupting her. "I'd better call the airline right now."

Mother met my eyes. "It's not going to be the way you think."

"Maybe. But then I'll know for myself what he's like, won't I?"

Mother shrugged. "Don't say I didn't warn you."

But this time I wasn't listening to her warnings.

"Since I'm going to visit Dad while he's in the hospital, I may stay awhile—a few days anyway," I said.

Mother made a face. "He won't agree to see you. I promise you, you're making a long trip for nothing."

"Of course he'll see me," I said sharply. "I'm his daughter."

"I know him better than you do, Liz."

But I could tell by the resignation in her voice that she had already accepted what I was going to do. I picked up the telephone and dialed the airline.

CHAPTER 2

My father was a patient at Memorial Hospital in a town called Duck Cove in North Carolina. My mother had learned this from Grandfather Herrick when she called to alert him that I planned to visit my father. I didn't expect to find an international airport in Duck Cove, but I was surprised by how hard it was to get to the place. No passenger trains went there, and the few buses that served the coast arrived at impossible times, like three in the morning. In the end I took the advice of my travel agent: I laid over in New York City one night, then flew down to Richmond, Virginia, and rented a car. The rental-car contract plainly said that renters had to be over twenty-one, but even though I showed the clerk my license, with my date of birth clearly stated on it, he never blinked. I signed the rental car agreement and went out to claim a little blue Geo Metro in the lot. It was as anonymous looking as a car could possibly be, which was fine with me.

Getting away from the Richmond airport was major stress. I hadn't done much driving since I got my license, and the tricky maneuvers, like left turns, still scared me. My palms were sweating and the steering wheel felt slippery in my hands. Once I was on I-95, I let out a sigh of relief. Long empty stretches of road were punctuated only by green signs for destinations and blue signs for "food, fuel, lodging." Those signs were the only clues to life near the four-lane highway. I might have been on the main road to hell.

I had to pay attention when I turned onto a narrow state road and headed toward Duck Cove on the Outer Banks. I found myself behind a slow-moving pickup filled with trash and old tires. I hadn't practiced passing on a two-lane road and was afraid to try it. It didn't help that I had to keep looking at the map. The road was crossed again and again by unnamed side roads, which made me wonder if I had missed a turn somewhere. Seedy shacks along the way had posted signs advertising surfboards and fish bait.

I began to notice seagulls wheeling overhead and knew I must be near the coast. The sky with its pale sun stretched hot and bright above me. I had the car's air conditioning on full blast. In England this temperature would have sent people to the hospital with heat prostration. The two-lane road cut between sandy hills with sparse patches of vegetation. The land was bleak, except for the inland tidal pools reflecting the sky.

At last I saw a sign saying "Welcome to Duck Cove." I stopped at the nearest gas station and bought a copy of the local newspaper. It had four sheets, most of them devoted to a recent fishing competition. I did find a brief story on page two about my twin's murder. "Local police have no leads in the recent robbery that ended in the death of Mary Hedrick, daughter of summer resident Dick Hedrick. Police caution residents to secure all doors and windows at night and not to open the door to visitors who cannot satisfactorily identify themselves." I smiled a little at the paper's creative rendition of our family name. And so far as I knew, Isabel never used the name Mary, though it was legally her first name—Isabel was her middle name. The reporter must have gotten it straight off her death certificate. And our last name was misspelled, to boot. I noticed that the little weekly paper was full of misprints.

I got directions to the county hospital, which turned out to be an ugly cement-block building surrounded by a black asphalt parking lot. I parked and got out. The heat of the pavement burned through the thin soles of my shoes. I stared at the squat, ugly building ahead of me, unable to move. I guess I was afraid of finding out what was inside the building. *Don't be silly,* I told myself. *The worst has already happened. Isabel is dead.*

I pushed open the hospital's glass doors and was hit with an arctic blast from the air conditioning. At the front desk, a woman in a pink jumper told me that visiting hours were over. An air of hushed silence pervaded the place, and I found myself lowering my voice. I explained that I was Richard Herrick's daughter, and that I had just flown over from Italy to see him. The pink lady's face melted into an expression of concern, and she urged me to go right on up.

At the nurse's station on the third floor, two nurses in crisp white were chatting about their recent car repairs. I had to clear my throat twice to get their attention. When I explained who I was, their faces immediately formed matching expressions of sympathy. One of the middle-aged women stood up at once and ushered me, with eerily silent footsteps, to my father's room.

I stepped into the room and saw my father lying limp on the hospital bed. If I hadn't seen the gentle movement of his breathing, I might have thought he was dead. His cheeks were sunken and the bones of his face stood out sharply, making him look a good deal older than his photo in *Contemporary Authors*. Flexible plastic tubes were taped to his arms, and a bottle of clear liquid hung suspended over one side of his bed.

His head turned, then his gray eyes widened at the sight of me. "Isabel," he whispered.

Goose bumps rose on my forearms. "I'm Liz," I said. "Not Isabel."

He stared at me as if he were trying to memorize my features.

"I'm not Isabel," I repeated firmly. "Don't start thinking of me as Isabel."

"Of course not." He licked his lips. "I can tell you're not Isabel."

"How?" I said quickly.

"How? Well, I know you can't be Isabel because Isabel is dead." His mouth worked.

"Were we very much alike?" I asked.

"Very," he said shortly.

"We were going to get together next year when we were at college. We were hoping we would get a chance to know each other then."

"Your voice is a bit lower than hers," he said.

"Really?" It had just occurred to me that there was a lot my father could tell me about Isabel.

"It's terrible," he said hoarsely. "Already I can't quite remember the sound of her voice."

I glanced around the room, a little surprised that it seemed so bare. Every hospital room I had ever visited had been filled with flowers. "Doesn't anyone know you're here?" I asked before I could stop myself.

He smiled sourly. "No. And that's the way I like it. The police notified my next of kin, but fortunately I regained consciousness soon enough to tell them to keep away. All I need is a bunch of family around here prattling about how famous I am, and the place will be swarming with reporters."

I glanced at him, startled. "You mean no one around here knows who you are?"

"I always tell people I'm in investments. That shuts them up." He snorted. "Nothing is more boring than investments."

I wondered if Duck Cove's library had copies of my father's books. Then, recalling the few, scattered houses and the forlorn gas station I had passed, I realized that the town probably didn't have a library. Duck Cove gave new meaning to the phrase "out of the way." I supposed that was what had drawn my father here.

"Tell me about yourself," he demanded suddenly. "Do you like games? Puzzles?"

He seemed disappointed when I said that I didn't.

"Maybe you read a lot, then?" he suggested.

I struck out on that count, too.

"You aren't a budding writer, evidently," he went on, not bothering to hide his disappointment.

"No. I guess I'm not." I watched him coolly. He might be my father, but he had never sent me so much as a birthday card, so it didn't bother me that he didn't like me. I figured he was no bargain either.

He snorted again. "So, how's your mother?" he asked abruptly. I followed his thinking: He was already blaming Mom for everything he didn't like about me.

"She's fine," I said. "She's talking about getting married in the spring."

"I feel deeply sorry for her fiancé." Suddenly, as if his dislike of Mother had given him an unexpected shot of energy, he sat up in bed and stabbed a finger against his buzzer. "I've got to get out of this place," he said. "Do you have a car?"

"I rented one in Richmond."

"You can drive me home, then," he said.

"You don't have your own car?"

"No," he said abruptly. "I was driving a rented one, and Isabel's car has disappeared."

A nurse came hurrying in. "Everything okay?" she asked brightly, her eyes darting anxiously from him to me.

"Take these tubes out of my arms," my father snapped. "I'm going home."

The nurse smiled at him as if he were a troublesome child. "I'll tell the doctor you're feeling much better, and we'll see what he says."

"Unhook this bottle or I'm going to go walking down the hall dragging it after me."

"It's a very serious matter to leave the hospital against medical advice." The nurse frowned, then in a solemn voice added the clincher: "If you leave against doctor's orders, your insurance may not pay!"

"I am leaving with or without your assistance,"

snapped Dad. "Iz—I mean, Elizabeth—get out of here while I put on some clothes."

I went out into the hall to wait for him. A couple of other people in white went in, and I could hear raised voices; eventually forms were brought for Dad to sign saying that he was leaving against medical advice. It never occurred to me to persuade him not to check out of the hospital. I could recognize determination when I saw it. Besides, I had to admit I was intrigued by the idea of going to Sewell's Falls. My father was bound to ask me to spend the night. Not only would I get to see where Isabel had lived, I might even get a chance to sleep in her room. I wondered if she had left a diary. If she had, I figured I would take it away with me. I had as much right to it as anyone.

It was odd to think that I had sat three feet from my father, looked into his eyes, and felt absolutely nothing. With Isabel it had been different. I barely remembered her—Had we played together in a sprinkler one hot afternoon or had I imagined it?—but even the mention of her name made my heart race. She was dead, but her name still called forth a rush of emotion. I was sure she was the one person in the world who could understand me. I needed her so badly that I still thought there was some way we could be close. I suppose this meant I was out of touch with reality, but that's the way it was.

When Dad came out of his room, he was short of breath. Even though he was in terrible shape, it was obvious to me that I had gotten my straight athletic-looking shoulders and the height that kept me from seeming fragile like my mother from him. My father was strongly built—but he was an ugly, forbidding-looking man with sallow skin and a prominent beaked nose. "They wanted to put me in a wheelchair," he barked. "I told them they could forget it. I'm perfectly capable of walking."

I didn't argue with him, but a wheelchair would have made sense. Even though I avoided looking at my father, I was conscious as we walked that he was unsteady on his feet.

The heat and light of the parking lot hit us when we stepped outside the big glass doors. Dad tottered a bit and blinked. Maybe I should have put out my arm to steady him, but I couldn't bring myself to touch him. When he slid into the car's passenger seat, I noticed that his lips were blue.

"Are you sure you're okay?" I asked.

He glared at me. "I'm as okay as can be expected, considering that I've had a heart attack and my daughter's been murdered. Any other questions?"

I leaned over him and pulled the map out of the glove compartment. "How far is it to Sewell's Falls?" I asked.

"About a three-hour drive," he said.

He was having a hard time taking his eyes off me. It was a trifle unnerving. I turned the car in the direction of the highway. "Tell me about Isabel."

He heaved a sigh. "It's impossible to sum her up in a couple of sentences. I know everything there is to know about her, you see. I wouldn't know where to begin."

I glanced at him out of the corner of my eye; there was no hint of irony in his expression. Maybe he *thought* he knew everything about Isabel. But everyone has secrets. In my seventeen years I had learned that much.

"Did she have a boyfriend?" I asked.

"Lots of them," he said promptly. "Boys ran after her constantly. But she was far too young to get involved. She enjoyed admiration, but she wasn't interested in anyone in particular." He dabbed at his eyes with a handkerchief.

He was kidding himself. Juliet had been younger than Isabel when she started sneaking out to see Romeo. "You mean there were no boys in her life at all?" I asked skeptically.

"Rob Blakely came around a lot. She liked him," he admitted. "I never could understand why. I think he was a lot more serious about her than she was about him. From the time she was five or six, I knew she was going to be a beauty. She could have her pick."

"We both look like Mom, I guess."

"Don't be ridiculous," he snapped. "Isabel didn't resemble Anne in the slightest."

Sure. Just because we were three blonds with dark eyebrows and identical short noses didn't mean we looked alike. "Was Isabel good at school?" I asked. I was terrific at school, mostly because I didn't have much else to do with my time.

"She was interested in *life*," he said. "She was a student of the human heart. She could have been a great writer—not that I ever tried to push her, but she had talent." He sighed. "Her hunger for life was magnificent. It was as if she knew she needed to scoop up experience because her time was short." He blotted his cheeks with his handkerchief. "Chess, computers, student government, music, art—so many interests. I know she was happy. That's my consolation." He closed his mouth abruptly.

Isabel sounded revoltingly like the well-rounded girl the college admissions committees wanted. I couldn't believe that was the whole story. Dad might have known Isabel, but I figured I knew her in a way he didn't. I was her twin.

"Tell me about what she was like when she was growing up," I suggested.

He didn't need encouragement. He told me about Isabel's life in so much detail you would have thought I was going to be the star in a movie about her. I learned that she had liked being the lead horsey in her pretend games at the playground when she was seven, that she had turned vegetarian at eight, and had gone back to eating beef at fourteen. It was strange hearing about Isabel's life, almost like encountering an alternate reality. Would I have turned out more like her if I had grown up in Sewell's Falls?

My father stared out the window blankly. "She was outgoing," he said, "not like me." His eyes glistened with tears. "She didn't know the meaning of fear. Went off the high-dive at six." He took his handkerchief out of his pocket again and blew his nose, then he turned accusing eyes on me. "You're not like her at all. I don't know what I expected. I was completely staggered when my father called and warned me you were coming. I suppose I had some half-insane idea you could replace Isabel. But you're different. You're cold."

I wasn't going to let him get away with that. "I don't even know you," I pointed out. "What did you expect?"

He snorted. "The trouble is, you're like *me*."

At last he had succeeded in offending me. We drove for the next hour in tight-lipped silence, and I began to wonder what I was getting myself into. The last thing I wanted was to get into a contest with my father in which I tried to prove I was as good as Isabel. Why should I care what he thought? He was as much a stranger to me as the man I sat next to on the plane. His opinion meant nothing to me.

Soon, however, I realized I had nothing to gain by letting him know how angry I was. If I got in a fight with him, all I would do is cut off a fountain of information about Isabel. "So, tell me about Isabel's friends," I said at last, breaking the silence.

"Everyone loved her," he said.

Naturally. That goes without saying, I thought ironically. He filled me in on everyone she had ever been close to. I listened carefully, but the entire time, I was wondering how I could find out what Isabel was *really* like. *A diary,* I thought. I didn't keep a diary myself, but Isabel had grown up with our father telling her every day that writing was more important than boys. Of course she would have kept a diary.

CHAPTER

By the time we drove up the winding lane to my father's house, I could have made a perfect score on a test about Isabel's life. That wasn't exactly careful planning on my part, but it turned out to be convenient.

The house was a two-story mock-Tudor building that was thickly surrounded by trees. No sign of neighbors. I thought I spotted a glimpse of a house hidden among the trees as we came up the long drive, but when I asked my father about it, I was told it was only the gazebo. "No neighbors for a mile on either side," he reported with some satisfaction. "We're tucked away in our own private Eden."

"It looks like a big house to keep up by yourself," I said.

31

"A housekeeping service comes in once a week," he said. "They don't know us—we don't know them. That's the way I like it. You'd better carry your own suitcase. You can stay in Isabel's room. The beds won't be made up in the guest room."

After what Mother had told me about him, I had expected a fortress complete with an electrified fence and Doberman pinschers. Instead my father's big house was indistinguishable from hundreds of others like it in prosperous suburbs.

He switched on the light in the living room; I saw a wall of books and a modern fireplace with a hearth of black tile and a length of polished wood over the mantel, both of which stretched up to the cathedral ceiling. I also saw at once that something was wrong. Gaps in the shelves gave the tall bookcases a snaggletoothed look. Books lay facedown on the carpet and were strewn all over the room. The cushions on the long sofa had been tossed to the floor and lay askew, one on top of the other. I glanced quickly at my father.

A cry escaped him as he strode quickly across the room and through the archway that led to the dining room. I heard the faint click of well-oiled metal. Then he appeared again, looking pale. "The deadbolt's still locked," he said. "I don't understand it. How did they get in?" He sank into a chair and put a hand to his chest as he struggled for breath.

"Maybe a sonic boom knocked the books down," I suggested.

He shot me a scornful look.

I stepped through the archway to the dining room. Like the living room, it was bleakly modern. A glass slab made up the top of the dining-room table. Glancing past the open kitchen door, I could see that the kitchen was undisturbed, so I returned to my father and reported that nothing seemed to be missing.

"Check my computer. See if they took it." My father gestured impatiently. "In my study—the other side of the hall."

I moved cautiously across the hall that bisected the house and opened a door on the other side of it. I carefully glanced around the good-sized study before I went in. The computer seemed untouched next to its printer, but papers had been flung everywhere and the desk chair was overturned. The intruder had ignored a lot of expensive computer equipment, I noticed. Here, as in the living room, his focus had been on ransacking books and papers. I went back to the living room to tell my father.

"The computer's still there," I said. "But somebody's messed up your papers. I think we'd better call the police before we go upstairs, just in case the burglar is still around."

He glared at me. "You call them, since *you're* so calm," he snapped. He was obviously furious that I wasn't as upset as he was. Maybe he even hated me for being young and healthy. It crossed my mind to wonder if he had resented Isabel as well. He praised her, but was there something a little phoney about it? It seemed odd to me that a writer would fall into clichés every time he spoke of his own daughter. Wouldn't he throw in an original phrase or a fresh image once or twice, even if only by accident?

I dialed the police and reported the break-in. "They're sending someone right away," I said as I hung up. Glancing at my father, I noticed that a sheen of sweat glistened on his face. "Do you have any medicine you ought to be taking?"

"I'm fine. I just need to sit down again for a few minutes." He pressed his hand to his chest and gasped.

A pair of policemen showed up at the door surprisingly soon. "You reported a burglary?" asked one of the officers.

I nodded. "I didn't want to go upstairs until you checked it out. Not that I really think the burglar's hiding in the shower or anything."

"Stranger things have happened," said the other officer, drawing his gun. The two policemen headed up the stairs. After a few minutes they came down again. "All clear," one announced. "But they've made quite a mess in your bedroom," he added, jerking his head toward me. "Somebody even took a knife to the mattress."

Dad gasped.

"My father's just out of the hospital after a heart attack," I explained. "He's not up to this."

The officer nodded understandingly. "It's a shock. Can you tell yet if anything is missing?"

"They didn't take the microwave or the computer," I said.

"Any jewelry, coin collection, fancy watches, things like that lying around?" asked the other officer. "They don't always like to mess around with the heavy stuff."

Dad shook his head. "I don't own anything like that."

The thin officer scratched his head and looked at me quizzically. "Got any disappointed boyfriends?" He took a deep breath. "I'll tell you the truth, miss. This doesn't look like your standard burglary. For one thing, I don't see how they got in."

Dad gaped at him, then slowly closed his mouth. "The keys. They must have had Isabel's keys."

"We just had a burglary at our beach house," I explained. For some reason I shied away from mentioning Isabel's death. "My father's thinking they could have gotten hold of the keys to the house then."

The officer's brow cleared. "That must be it. Happens all the time. They snatch some lady's purse and next thing you know they've hit the house, too. You'd better call yourself one of those twenty-four-hour locksmiths and get your locks changed." He glanced at Dad, who was white and shaken. "In fact," he went on, "we'll call them for you. Maybe something scared them off and that's why they didn't finish the job. Could be that they heard you drive up."

"I'm going upstairs to take a look," I said suddenly.

"I better go with you," said the officer. "Lots of folks can't take it when burglars trash the house. Last week we had a lady keel over on us in a dead faint."

Not taking the time to explain that I wasn't the fainting type, I charged upstairs. I spotted Isabel's room right away. It faced the top of the stairs and its door was open so that I could see a black and purple poster on the wall that proclaimed "Expresso Yourself." Even though I had been braced for disorder, the wholesale destruction of her room took my breath away. Shredded pillows lay on the ripped sheet, and the mattress was crooked on its box spring. The bedclothes had been flung off the bed, and the mattress ripped open. All the books lay heaped together on the floor. The drawers of Isabel's desk had been flung open, and her pens and paper clips were strewn all over the flowered rug. Shoe boxes, their contents spilling out, had been tossed out of the closet, and some were crushed, as if they had been stepped on by a heavy foot.

An elaborate chess set lay overturned, its pieces scattered. I picked up one of the pieces. At first I thought it was a black king, since a tiny crown sat askew on its head. But the king in this set was a dragon. His webbed tail was wrapped halfway around his haunches, and his jaws were wide open, showing white teeth and a lick of its forked red tongue. The small dragon was exquisite; a work of art. I picked up the black knight next, a medieval knight in full armor. His visor was up and underneath were the painted features of a skull. The black knight was Death! I sucked in my breath involuntarily. Part of a rook, a round tower to judge by similar pieces, had been ground almost to powder under the prowler's angry heel. Now I saw why the officer had suggested that a disappointed boyfriend might have trashed the room. The damage was savage, vindictive, and somehow personal.

The officer regarded me sympathetically. "Rotten time for this to happen with school starting tomorrow morning. Tell you what, why don't my partner and me get this bed out of here and bring in a bed from the empty room across the hall? Then at least you'll have a place to sleep tonight."

I licked my lips. "Thank you," I said. I realized that the policeman thought I was Isabel. It didn't seem worthwhile explaining that I wasn't.

When I came downstairs, my father's eyes sought mine anxiously. "How bad is it?" he asked.

I shrugged. "Pretty much everything can be fixed."

He looked away from me. "I don't think I'll try to go upstairs tonight."

"That's the best thing, sir," one of the officers assured him. "You take it easy."

My father's bedroom adjoined his study, so there was no hope of concealing the damage there from him. "What's the point of it?" he said, looking around at the disheveled papers strewn over the floor. "It doesn't matter that they've thrown the manuscript around. I've got the entire thing on a disk." He switched the computer on, then clicked it off as soon as it booted up. "The destruction is so senseless."

"You'd better go to bed," I said. "I'll wait for the locksmith. Do you have a phone in your room so you can call if you need help?"

"I'll be fine," he said.

His bedroom, at least, was undisturbed. I saw that the bed was neatly made up with a twill bedspread. Books were everywhere in random stacks on the floor, and they looked as if they had been laying there for weeks. I could see the marks of a carpet sweeper in neat squares around them. The housecleaning service must be under orders not to move them. Except for the stacks of books, the place was very neat. An anorexic heron with wispy feathers was framed over the dresser, looking disapprovingly down at a set of silver combs and brushes. Beside it was a painting of a raven, its shoulders hunched. The evil-eyed bird reminded me uncomfortably of my father, and I had to force my eyes away from it.

"Can I get you anything before I go?" I asked him. "Water? Medicine?"

He shook his head. "I'm okay."

But as I reached the door, he said suddenly, "Liz, why don't you try living here with me for a while?"

I was thrown off balance by the unexpected offer.

"Just for a little while," he added. "You don't have to leave yet, do you?"

"No. Not exactly."

"Then why not stay?"

"I'll think it over," I said slowly.

"Do that." He sat down suddenly on the bed. "I feel a little dizzy. I think I'll lie down."

I found the two police officers waiting for me in the living room.

"Your dad looks pretty shaken up," said the officer who had come with me upstairs.

"He only just got out of the hospital," I explained.

The other officer looked around the room.

"Never thought I'd get a call out here. Everybody knows how your dad likes to keep to himself—our famous writer." He lowered his voice. "I hear he never gives any interviews or anything. Even gets his groceries delivered."

The first officer piped up, "I don't think you know her, but my daughter's in your class at school. Cassie Wiggins. Cassie's always telling me you're a real popular girl."

The doorbell rang and I jumped a mile.

"That'll be the locksmith," said Officer Wiggins.

I was still trying to process my father's surprising offer to live with him. Really, there was no reason why I couldn't. I had already passed the International Baccalaureate, which was all I needed to get into the colleges I planned to apply to. I had figured on having a year off before starting college.

The officers left as soon as the locksmith showed up. The man took out a huge electric drill and set to work at once. Over the noise of the drill, I caught the first ring of the telephone and grabbed the receiver.

"Hello?" I said.

"Liz? I can hardly hear you. What's that noise?"

"Just a minute. Let me move to the kitchen phone." I took the receiver off the hook in the kitchen, then ran back and replaced the other one in its cradle in the living room. Next I rushed breathlessly back to the kitchen. All the while I was wondering who could possibly have traced me to Sewell's Falls, North Carolina.

"Okay," I panted. "This'll be better. The locksmith is making a terrific racket in there."

"What's a locksmith doing at your house?"

"Who is this?" I asked, puzzled.

"Jane!" she cried indignantly. "Who'd you think?"

I leafed madly through the file cards of my mind trying to remember all the Janes I had ever known. Could it be Jane Grignon? But why would she be calling me? I hadn't seen her since we shared a room on a ski trip last winter.

"Iz, I've missed you so much! I'm going crazy glued to the house all summer! I thought you were supposed to be home ages ago. Where have you been? I called the beach house yesterday heaps of times, morning, noon, and night; so then I thought, well, you must be home, but when I called the house—nothing."

Iz, not Liz! This girl thought she was speaking

to Isabel! I realized that my father's obsession with privacy had kept the news of Isabel's death from getting back to Sewell's Falls. "Dad's had a heart attack," I explained, wondering how to break the news. "He's been in the hospital." I was going to have to tell this girl about Isabel. What should I say?

"Gosh! Is he okay?" she asked quickly.

"More or less," I said evasively. "But listen— there's something I've got to tell you."

"I've got a million things to tell you. A trillion. I can't believe it, but I'm actually glad school's starting tomorrow. If I don't get out of this house soon, I'm going to go stark raving mad. I'll pick you up at eight. Oh, no! Mom's calling for me. I know it's not her fault, but she's driving me crazy. I've got to go, Iz. See you tomorrow."

She hung up before I had a chance to explain. I stood staring at the phone, wondering who on earth I had been talking to. Isabel's best friend, I supposed. I remembered now that my father had said Jane Crumpler and Isabel were inseparable. At first when she said "Iz," I had thought she said "Liz." I hadn't realized Isabel's friends shortened her name. How strange! I fished out the phone book and checked the listing for Crumpler. No luck. They must have an unlisted number.

The locksmith stood at the kitchen door. "That'll take care of it." He held out his grease-smeared palm and handed me four shiny new keys. "That's a hundred and fifty dollars. An extra fifty because it was an emergency call after regular hours."

"My father's gone to bed. Would it be possible for you to bill us?"

"Sure thing. I know you're good for it." He took a black notebook out of his hip pocket and jotted something down. "Richard Herrick, right?" He smiled at me, showing even white teeth.

"That's right."

"I work days at Bryson's Chevrolet. This is just my night job. Your new car's come in, and you can pick it up tomorrow."

"Oh!" I stared at him. "That's . . ." It was too complicated to explain. "Thank you," I finished lamely.

I locked the doors carefully when he left, then went upstairs. The police had dragged Isabel's mutilated bed into the guest room across the hall and pulled the guest-room bed into her room.

I went into Isabel's room, closed the door, and leaned against it, surveying the mess with dismay. In a minute I would need to find linens and make up the bed. I carefully picked up the chess pieces off the floor and put them on the desk. It was a beautiful set, each of the pieces a tiny work of art. The crushed rook was beyond repair, but I brushed up the broken bits with my fingers and laid them on the desk with the rest of the set. I picked up a few books off the floor and put them back in the sleek white bookcase. *Anne of Green Gables. The Hitchhiker's Guide to the Galaxy. Native Son. One Writer's Story* by Eudora Welty. A stack of sleazy magazines were strewn by the bookcase—*Unsolved Crimes*. I stacked them neatly. The issue on top showed a woman tied to a chair, her mouth open in a terrified scream. I shivered and turned the cover facedown. Evidently, Isabel had had a strong stomach.

I glanced around the room curiously. It hit me suddenly that this room, unlike the two ransacked rooms downstairs, had no papers strewn about. Odd. I pulled open the large drawer to the filing cabinet and found several years worth of old English papers neatly filed. But conspicuously absent were letters from friends, diaries, notebooks.

Isabel's desk was unusual. Its top was inlaid with wood in the pattern of a checkerboard, and around the edges of the writing surface was an ornate facing with more inlaid wood depicting chess pieces and the suits of cards. It had only narrow and shallow drawers down one side, and I realized that it must be a converted game table. The drawers, impractical for filing paper, had probably been designed for holding small game pieces. It looked as if Isabel had kept paper clips and staples in them.

The phone beside the bed rang shrilly. I picked it up in mid-ring, hoping that my father had thought to unplug the one in his room so the ring wouldn't wake him.

"Hello?"

"Liz?"

"This is Elizabeth," I responded cautiously, not quite sure whether the caller had asked for me or Isabel.

"It's Mother, darling. Are you all right?"

I exhaled. "Oh! Yeah, sure, I'm fine." I was so relieved it wasn't one of Isabel's friends that I felt limp.

"You could have called to let me know you'd arrived all right," she complained. "I was petrified your father was going to pick up the phone, but I had to check and make sure you were all right."

"What did you think? That he'd murdered me?"

"Don't joke about that, Liz. It isn't funny."

"Dad has asked me to stay for a while, and I'm thinking it over. Maybe I will."

"You mean, stay in Sewell's Falls? What would you do there?"

"I'd go to school, I guess."

"There must be something wrong with this connection," Mother said crossly. "I thought you said you were planning to go to school in Sewell's Falls."

"How am I going to meet anybody my own age if I don't go to school?"

"Honestly, Liz, this is absurd. It doesn't make a bit of sense. If you go to the local high school, you are going to be bored out of your mind."

I smiled to myself. "I don't think I'll be bored."

"Listen, darling, I have a wonderful idea! Simon's nephew is going to go backpacking in Thailand. You could go with him. Don't you think that sounds like fun?"

"No. I think I'll give this a try. I'll give you a call in a week or so and let you know how it's going."

"Don't bother!" she said crossly. "I won't have to be told how it's going. It's going to be a perfect disaster. Has your father done anything unutterably weird yet?" I could hear the undercurrent of anxiety in her voice.

"Not yet. Maybe he'll do better once he gets his strength back."

"Don't tease me, Elizabeth," she said. "Vera Wallace wants me to go along on a cruise. Her tiresome sister has got the flu and she wants me to fill in for her. Now I'll have to worry about you the entire time. Thanks a lot."

I could just picture it—Mother sunning herself on the deck of a Greek ship and worrying herself sick about me. *Right.*

"Sorry," I said. "But this is something I've got to do."

"You're going to regret it," she said.

She was probably right. I knew it was a crazy idea. But at the same time I had to give it a try. Staying around Sewell's Falls for a while was now the only way I could get close to Isabel.

After I hung up, my eyes rested on the bookshelves over the bed. They were filled with games—lots of them. The shelves held several boxes of playing cards and a wide collection of board games—Strategy, Scrabble, Clue, Battle, and one I didn't recognize that had polished gems for pieces. I had no idea how to play most of them. The last game I had played with any seriousness was hopscotch.

Scanning them, I could see that Isabel's taste ran to puzzle-type games. So I wasn't a bit surprised to pick up off the floor a collection of old *New York Times* crossword puzzles, half-filled out, and a huge crossword-puzzle dictionary. I put the books away and stashed the shoe boxes back in the closet. With all the boxes and books stowed away, the room began to look more normal.

I opened the door beside the desk and found myself looking into the adjoining bathroom. I was pleased to find it untouched—no nasty words scrawled on the mirror, no spilled shampoo. The drawer to the bathroom vanity held a few lipsticks, some old barrettes, combs, brushes, and boxes of strawberry soap. Under the sink I found a collection of shampoos and hair conditioners. Isabel hadn't worn much makeup, I concluded, but she had been proud of her hair. I glanced in the mirror, raising my eyebrows a bit as I saw myself. It gave me an odd feeling to think that Isabel must have stood here many times looking at virtually the same image in the mirror. I had no idea how she had worn her hair, but mine fell to my shoulders, straight and blond except for the slight crinkle of a curl at my left temple.

I knew I needed to get the bed made up, but I wasn't sure where to find linens. A quick check in the bathroom closet showed plenty of fluffy towels but no sheets. A linen closet had to be around somewhere. I went out into the hall and checked the other doors. In addition to the guest room, there was a bedroom and bath on the other side of the stairs. Down the hall in the other direction was a narrow door that proved to be the linen closet. I carried an armful of sheets back to Isabel's room and made up the bed. Then I unpacked my suitcase and put on my favorite old pajamas. The elastic at the waist had long ago given way, and I held them up with a safety pin.

I had been certain I wouldn't sleep a wink, but I had forgotten what a long day it had been. Once I got in bed and pulled the covers up to my chin, I was out cold. I was so tired that even though I heard the buzz of an alarm in the middle of the night, I could not make myself move. The buzzing finally stopped, and the darkness of sleep closed over me again.

CHAPTER 4

I heard a honk outside and jumped. When I parted the living-room curtains, I saw a battered Camaro poised in the driveway, its motor running.

"That's my ride," I said nervously. My heart was pounding in my throat. What was I so afraid of? Not that it was going to be easy to tell Jane that Isabel was dead—it would be hard. It would be even harder if Jane took it as some kind of joke and refused to believe me, but I was ready for that. I had my driver's license tucked into the pocket of my jeans as proof of who I was.

My father passed his fingers over his closed eyelids in a gesture of great weariness. "Glad you decided to stay, Iz—Elizabeth. I think I'm just going to lie down a minute before I get to work."

"Good idea," I said. "I'll see you after school." I darted out the door and then walked hesitantly toward the Camaro. To my astonishment, the rear door of the car flew open and a tall boy jumped out. I recoiled as he grabbed my shoulders.

"Iz," he said hoarsely, "I know I'm the last person you're expecting to see, but I've got to talk to you."

"I'm not . . ." I began, but looking into his black-lashed hazel eyes, I couldn't make myself go on.

A girl with flyaway auburn hair stuck her head out the car window. "Not here, Rob. You're going to have Iz's dad charging out the door yelling at us. Get in the car."

"We've got to talk," he repeated, his hands dropping to his sides. "It's important."

I swallowed. "I . . . all right. Later."

He shot me a grateful look and jumped back into the car. I scrambled in next to him.

"Drive, Jeeves," he said in a deep voice.

Jane jerked the car into reverse. It was at that moment that it occurred to me how easy it would be to let them go on thinking I was Isabel. Rob was sneaking looks at me, but I pretended not to notice. In the tight quarters of the backseat, we were close enough that I could feel the heat of his body. He smelled clean, as if he had just got out of the shower, and I could see the comb marks running through his damp hair.

I leaned my head back against the seat cushions. If I broke the news of Isabel's death now, I knew her friends would immediately drop out of my life. After the first wave of disbelief and grief had washed over them, they would look at me uncomfortably from a distance, reminded of Isabel's death. They'd probably end up behaving like my father, as if I were some strange sort of half-person who happened to look like Isabel. I would never know their secrets or touch the part of their lives they had shared with her. I would be an outsider and a curiosity. Suddenly I knew I could not resist the temptation to let them think I was Isabel. It was the one way I could try to reclaim my lost twin.

"Iz," Jane spoke over her shoulder, "who did you get for physics?"

"I'm not sure," I said.

"Didn't you get the list of your courses in the mail?" asked Rob.

"I don't think so," I said.

Jane grumbled. "The mail delivery around here is ridiculous. They must have sent them out in

July or something. Yours probably got forwarded to the beach cottage and was lost."

"Very probably."

Jane stiffened. "Are you all right, Iz?"

I cleared my throat. "Fine. Why do you ask?"

"You sound funny. Doesn't she sound funny, Rob?"

He grinned. "She sounds great to me." A guilty look swept over him. I wished I knew how to interpret it. I realized it was going to be tricky for me to know how to behave with him. For one thing, I didn't know exactly what sort of relationship he had had with Isabel.

"We're seniors!" cried Jane, flinging a freckled arm out the car window. "We're on top! Just one more year and it's look out world—here we come! Can you believe it?" She glanced back over her shoulder and I saw that her face was open and friendly. I was sure she would be the last person to suspect that I was not who I seemed to be. She had the look of someone who always expected the best from people. "It's so great to have you back, Iz. It's been dull, dull, dull without you."

"The Shnecks broke up. That's one bit of news I bet you haven't heard yet." Rob glanced at me. "Aren't you surprised?"

I shrugged. "It happens."

"But the *Shnecks*!" screeched Jane. "They were, like, glued together. And catch the reason—Lisa caught him cheating on her!"

"Imagine that!" I said. By now it was easy for me to guess how I was supposed to react, and I raised my eyebrows in surprise.

"Just the thought of touching Schroeder—*ugh*—I'd as soon kiss a slug," said Jane. "Who's the girl he was fooling around with, Rob?"

"I think she goes to some other school."

"But here's the weird thing—Lisa is so much more attractive since she broke up with him. She's gotten outgoing and bouncy. You remember how they used to sort of cling damply together—well, she's totally different now."

"Not totally," Rob demurred.

"She's going around with this new boy, Pete." Jane lowered her voice dramatically. "And Rob's already seen them making out."

"Yup," said Rob with morbid satisfaction, "I think what's next on the agenda is—can I say it?—the Pnecks!"

I caught on that neither Schroeder nor Lisa were actually named Schneck or Pneck. The made-up names were in-jokes that must refer to their habit of necking in public. I hoped Isabel's friends didn't go in big for that sort of wordplay. Pretending to be Isabel was going to be hard enough. I would be completely lost if her friends started talking in code.

The intersection ahead was marked with a sign pointing to Sewell's Falls High School, and I felt my spine stiffen. We joined a line of cars on a road that wound through pinewoods. I knew that American teenagers went for cars in the same enthusiastic way Italian kids went for motor scooters, but I hadn't quite visualized what this would mean when it came to traffic. I spotted a teacher standing beside the road speaking into a walkie-talkie. It looked as if she were put there to keep the cars from ramming each other in frustration. We inched slowly ahead.

"As soon as Dad gets back from this leadership workshop he's at, he's going to take some kids on a canoe trip," Jane said. "It's for incoming transfer students—sort of an extra orientation effort for the super lost." Jane glanced over her shoulder. "I figured we'd all go with them. Maybe I'll meet some cool new guys. Besides, it's such great weather lately for canoeing."

"Sure, we can go," I said, "but you'll have to teach me to canoe."

They both stared. Belatedly it hit me that I shouldn't have volunteered that I didn't know how to canoe. Presumably Isabel did. I smiled. "I mean, I feel like I'd be starting all over, and I'm not sure I'm up to a wilderness trek. A few days ago the beach house got broken into, and the robbers knocked me out. Sometimes I still get kind of woozy and confused."

"You mean you got attacked?" cried Jane.

"Jeez!" breathed Rob. "That's horrible. You could have been killed!"

I touched my forehead with my fingertips. My thoughts of Isabel were so strong that I felt a painful pressure there, as if she were inside me. "It was scary," I said. "I'm still having some memory problems." It occurred to me it would be a good idea to make a big deal about how bad my "concussion" had been. It might come in handy as an excuse for possible slips. But Rob looked so alarmed that I hastened to add, "I'm okay, really."

"What about your dad?" cried Jane. "Was he there when it happened? Was he hurt?"

I shook my head. "He had gone to Richmond. When he came back and found me laid out cold on the floor, he barely had time to call 911 before he collapsed." I closed my eyes. The scene as it

must have occurred was vivid in my imagination—
Isabel's face unrecognizably bloodied, the flies
buzzing in the silent room. My mouth had gone
dry and it was hard to shut the terrible image out
of my mind. "He was in pretty bad shape after
that, and the doctors say he needs to take it easy."

Rob's hand brushed against mine. My hand
jerked, and I found myself meeting his gaze. He
had straight dark brows that were uneven where a
thin scar ran through one of them. His jaw was
broad and his chin was shadowed with a cleft. But
it wasn't any of these things that caught my
attention. It was something in the way the
atmosphere between us was charged. "Did they
catch the guy who did it?" he asked in a low voice.

"What?" I stared at him.

"The burglar."

"Oh." I felt hot color rush to my face. "No,
they haven't caught him yet. I couldn't give them a
description or anything. That whole day is pretty
much a blank, actually."

"And it happened at the beach!" breathed
Jane. "You'd think you'd be okay there, but it
seems like nobody's safe anywhere anymore."

"Did they get away with much?" asked Rob.

I shrugged. "Some cash and my car."

"You were getting ready to sell the car, anyway, so that's not so bad," said Jane. "The insurance will pay you something for it."

"If the police have a description of the car, that might help them catch the guys," added Rob.

I became aware that the air outside the car's windows had become brighter. The woods around us were thinning. Glancing ahead I saw a complex of brick buildings connected by cement walkways and drives. Too bad I hadn't had a chance to look the high school over ahead of time. Isabel would have known her way around blindfolded, but I would be seeing everything for the first time. And I would need to find my way without letting anyone realize how confused I was.

As we drew closer to the cluster of buildings, I saw what looked like a seething carnival of brightly dressed kids. I realized suddenly that I didn't know which of them Isabel knew and which she didn't. That meant I would be snubbing friends right and left without realizing it. Jane's car pulled up into a circular drive in front of a large building that looked as if it might hold an auditorium. I tensed. What had ever made me think I could pull this off?

"I hate the first day of school." Rob was peering out the window. "Everywhere you look you see freshmen about to burst into tears."

"If they're lost, that's their problem," crowed Jane. "We were lost and confused when we were freshmen. Now it's their turn." Her car slowed down and stopped next to a No Parking sign. "I'll let you off here, Iz, since you've got to go to the office and get your schedule." She grinned. "I'm going to go and get in on the seniors' celebration in the parking lot. Seniors forever— yea!" She blew several sharp taps on her horn. Cars behind us sounded answering blasts.

I climbed out and was struck by the blazing sunshine and heat rising from the concrete. What I needed was a minute or two alone to pull myself together, so I was dismayed when Rob got out with me. I would have preferred for him not to watch me fumble around. He placed a hand firmly between my shoulder blades. "I'm going with you as far as the office," he said.

"You don't have to do that," I protested.

"What did the doctor say about that memory loss, Iz?" A worried crease had formed between his brows. "Does he think it's going to go away?"

"Probably. It's different for different people. It's nothing serious. Really."

I saw an arrow clearly marking the way to the

office, so I turned confidently in that direction. But all the time I was aware of the pressure of Rob's hand on my back. Kids were milling around the sidewalk in confusion, and the scene felt alien, as if I had been plunged into a bazaar in the Middle East. I was reminded of the time my mother and I had timidly ventured into the Khan Kahili market in Cairo. Today the sights and sounds were just as new to me, but I was more excited than scared. *I like this,* I thought, to my surprise. *This is fun.*

A girl with elaborately beaded corn rows trailing down her back walked past, her chin held high. We moved past a couple of guys who were tossing dimes against a brick wall, their faces blank with concentration. A guy with a mustache approached us, his brown hair falling in loose curls over his eyes so that he looked less like a kid than a friendly forest animal. "Hi, Iz." He grinned.

"Hi!" I said, startled.

Rob's firm hand pushed me forward as I tried to sneak glances at the kids around me. I looked up and saw that a big sheet was suspended overhead like a banner and painted with a crude cartoon of two kids in sunglasses—an over-muscled boy and a girl in a bikini who was carrying a boom box. The caption read "Senior Men, Senior Women." I deduced that the first day of school was when the seniors strutted their stuff. The vaguely depressed-looking kids we were passing on the walkway must have been underclassmen.

"A grisly spectacle, huh?" said Rob. "Everywhere you look you see stuck-up kids, put-down kids, kids afraid of being left out, kids afraid of being found out."

I stiffened, wondering what he had meant by that remark about kids afraid of being found out.

Rob shook his head "Another thing I hate about the first day of school is seniors acting full of themselves. Let's both run away and join the Foreign Legion."

"Do we have to send them our SAT scores?" I asked lightly. Somewhere a trumpet sounded, and I could hear shouts in the distance. That must be the seniors' celebration in the parking lot that Jane had mentioned.

Some kids in T-shirts painted with their class years came careening past us. Rob frowned. "I wish I could come on the second day and miss the craziness. I'll go all day thinking I'm going to get hit in the face with a water balloon."

Standing nearby was a clutch of girls with

unwashed hair. They wore platform sandals and layers of overlapping shirts and skirts that looked as if they were in the process of oozing slowly to the ground. I stared, then self-consciously looked away. Isabel wouldn't have given them a second glance, I realized. I knew I should try to avoid looking around curiously. "It's such a weird sensation being back at school." I laughed. "I feel like I'm seeing everything for the first time."

"You're giving me the creeps, Iz," Rob said. "Are you sure you're okay? I know you want me to butt out, but I can't help worrying about you. You could have gotten killed in that stupid burglary. Why'd your father have to get some beach cottage in the middle of nowhere and then go off and leave you by yourself?"

"He couldn't have guessed somebody would break into the house," I said. "It didn't even make sense." Isabel's death *didn't* make sense. Car thieves out among the sand dunes? A break-in while the beach house was occupied?

"Things that don't make sense happen all the time," said Rob.

I glanced at him. I had never been so aware of anyone in my life. He was taller than I, with broad shoulders. Though only his fingers pressed against my back, urging me on, I was very conscious of his closeness.

He spun me around suddenly to face him, grabbed my hands, and held them tight as if he were afraid I were going to run from him. "I know what you're going to say," he said. "I know that it's over between us, but I just wanted to tell you that I've broken up with Amy Rose."

I looked at him blankly. Amy Rose? Who was she? I was caught off balance.

"Well, aren't you going to say anything?" he demanded.

"I don't know what to say," I said blankly.

"Okay." His mouth twisted in disappointment. "Forget it, then. I just wanted you to know, that's all."

He turned away from me. On impulse I reached out and touched him. "Rob! Don't go."

He wheeled around. "What did you say?"

I gulped. "Just don't disappear from my life altogether, okay?"

He grinned suddenly, showing a flash of white teeth. "No danger. Look, I'll call you tonight, okay?"

I nodded.

When he had gone, I realized with a start that

I was standing in front of a door labeled OFFICE. Getting a copy of my schedule seemed suddenly irrelevant. I had bigger worries. It was clear that I had no idea what I was getting myself into. So Isabel had broken up with Rob. She must have had her reasons. I wished I knew what they were.

Belatedly I realized that I was staring at a 3-x-5 card thumbtacked to a nearby bulletin board:

A gathering of the Coven
2 A.M., Wednesday
Double double, toil and trouble.
—Madame Eglantine

Other students were streaming past me into the office, apparently unaware of the discreet, typed announcement thumbtacked to the board. It crossed my mind that for all I knew witches were commonplace around here.

I went into the office and joined a bunch of kids standing in a cluster in front of the counter. At last my turn came. "Your name?" asked the secretary.

My heart stopped. "Isabel Herrick," I said. It was a name close to my own—yet still it was hard to stretch my lips around it. "I—I need a new copy of my course schedule," I stuttered. "Mine never arrived."

The woman pulled a card out of a folder and handed it to me. I snatched a ground plan of the school from a stack on the counter and moved outside.

"Hey, there, stuck up!"

I felt a jab in my ribs and looked up startled to find Jane standing before me.

"Hi," I said. "I got my schedule."

Jane made a face. "All I got was an awful parking place. I'm practically jammed up against the power station, and I had to drive over fifty yards of gravel. I think seniors ought to get the best parking places, don't you? Somebody ought to get a petition going. You do it, Iz! You're good at that kind of thing."

"Not me." I shook my head. "Why don't you?"

"You know I can't because of my dad. I'll bet you'll be dying to do it once you start driving your Corvette. Wait till the gravel starts messing up your shiny new paint job."

I blinked in surprise. The car waiting at the dealership was a Corvette? It looked as if my twin hadn't shared my dislike of being conspicuous. My heart sank a little when I realized that I would be stuck with driving her flashy car whether I liked it or not. If I traded it in, everyone who knew Isabel would think I was acting very odd, and that was the last thing I wanted.

Jane gave me a smile and vanished. I took a deep breath, glanced at the map I had sneaked from the office, and headed toward the class marked on my schedule as HMRM.

Kids waved to me cheerfully as I passed them, and it gave me a queasy feeling to realize that I hadn't the faintest notion who they were. Luckily, finding my way around the school wasn't as tough as I had thought it would be. I had the help of the school map and also of the signs put up for freshmen. It was dealing with people that was going to be the problem.

Coming around a corner with my eyes fixed on my map, I collided with a boy with a white mop of curly hair who looked as if he could audition for a part as one of the Marx brothers. "Hey, Iz, who've you got for physics?" he asked.

I remembered. "Kolena."

"Hey, me too." He brightened.

He seemed to be expecting me to say more, so I ventured, "How was your summer?"

"Great. Got a job lifeguarding, saved some

money. What about you?"

"It was good," I said. I could tell from the way he was behaving that he wasn't a close friend of Isabel's, so I started to move away.

"Hey, Iz," he began.

I hesitated.

He blushed. "Oh, never mind." He thrust his hands in his pockets and fled.

I realized that it would be a help if I could learn some names and faces. I would have to spend the evening studying Isabel's yearbook.

"Hmrm" turned out to be a short period during which a teacher read out announcements. There were lots of them, but I seemed to be the only person paying attention.

I could relax during my first-period physics class because Mr. Kolena did all the talking. But as soon as the bell rang at the end of the period and the kids surged out into the hallway, I snapped into a state of hyper-alertness. I was so afraid of offending someone, I smiled constantly like the hostess on a game show.

At lunchtime I found my way to the cafeteria, but there I stopped, momentarily stymied. At every school I had ever known, kids ate with the same group of friends every day. Unfortunately, not only didn't I have a clue who Isabel's lunch bunch was, I didn't even know where they usually sat. I was thinking about skipping lunch to avoid this looming pitfall, when suddenly Jane appeared and swept me in the door with her.

A traffic bottleneck had formed just inside the cafeteria's double doors, and I felt kids' hot breath on me as we squeezed through. I was conscious of a dizzying confusion of jeans and T-shirts, and the noise of voices pitched to a shrill screech.

"Did you and Rob talk yet?" Jane asked.

"Not much." I snapped to attention. This would be tricky. Jane might not be suspicious, but she would know all kinds of little things about Isabel that other people wouldn't. Right now she was looking straight at me, and I realized, with a sudden contraction of my heart, that she was expecting me to share some sort of intimate secret. "Rob told me he broke up with Amy Rose," I offered

She smiled, apparently satisfied. "He's still hung up on you, Iz."

A faint cloud of steam met us as we moved into the cafeteria line.

"Can you see yourself getting back together with Rob?" asked Jane.

"It's better for us to be just friends." I slid a

plastic tray off a stack. "Friends" sounded safe enough.

Jane snorted. "Nobody's ever pulled off going back to being friends after they've been as close as you two."

Exactly how close was that? I wondered.

Behind the counter, a woman wearing a hair net plopped a metal dish of baked beans into a slot on the steam table. The air was stifling. I lifted the weight of my long hair off my neck with one hand and took a deep breath. I might look like Isabel and sound like her, but I felt that I was walking a tightrope blindfolded.

"It's just not possible to backtrack in a relationship." Jane dropped a dish of coleslaw onto her tray with a clatter. "Think about it, Iz. Too much has happened between you two."

A trail of sweat trickled down my back. I longed to know exactly what had happened between Isabel and Rob.

Lifting my tray, I carried it into the cafeteria proper.

"Do you see Kaki or Melissa anywhere?" Jane shouted in my ear.

"No." I stared hopelessly at the sea of strange faces before us.

"There they are! Good grief, Isabel, you're looking right at them!" cried Jane. "Don't you see them?"

I focused suddenly on the table directly ahead of us and was startled to be met by an obviously hostile look. A boy wearing a jeans vest and T-shirt was glaring at me. His mustard-colored hair was parted in the middle and hung straight to his ears.

"I think Carl is still ticked about the way you treated Rob," Jane hissed in my ear.

Great. Lunch should be heaps of fun with Carl looking daggers at me. Reluctantly I followed Jane to the table. My initial reaction when I sat down was mild vertigo, because the two girls sitting with Carl looked alike. Both had big smiles that showed their teeth all the way back to the molars, and both wore their dark hair cropped short and pushed behind their ears. Melissa and Kaki, I remembered Jane had called them. The only difference I could make out between them was that one wore tiny jade earrings and the other wore thin gold hoops.

"Are you okay, Iz?" One of them bent a head toward me anxiously.

"I told Kaki about the burglary," explained Jane.

Kaki was the one with jade earrings, so Melissa wore the gold hoops. Surely I could keep that much straight. "I'm pretty much okay," I said. I could feel my blouse sticking to my damp skin. "I'm having a little trouble, but I'm not sure if that's from the blow on the head or whether I'm having some kind of post-traumatic stress symptom."

"How awful!" Melissa said with a shudder.

"It must be hard for you to feel safe after something like that," said Kaki.

Maybe Kaki and Melissa didn't actually look alike after all. Maybe it was only that my brain was overworked from trying to keep straight all of the people I'd run into that morning. The safest thing to do, I realized, was to let the others do the talking and to concentrate on my food: a pink hot dog in a cold bun; shreds of pale cabbage and pink carrots in watery mayonnaise.

"You don't seem like yourself, Iz," Kaki said. "You're awfully quiet."

"She's had a bad shock," said Melissa. "How's your dad doing?"

"As well as can be expected," I said.

They clucked their tongues sympathetically.

"Oh, look!" cried Melissa. "Here comes Rob."

Both girls sneaked glances at me to check my reaction. Isabel's breakup with Rob would be common knowledge, of course.

"It's cool, guys," said Jane airily. "Rob and Iz are friends now."

Rob slid in across from me and smiled. "I am going to flunk calculus, you guys."

"Did you get Harkness?" cried Melissa. "He's really hard. He gave my brother a D."

Rob made a face. "Yeah. I didn't understand a word he said today, and all he was doing was going over the course outline."

"You ought to get a tutor," said Melissa. "That's what my brother says he wishes he had done. Who did you get, Iz?"

"I'm not sure."

"You haven't even looked?" cried Kaki. "I can't believe you! Boy, I wish I had that kind of confidence!"

I almost laughed. I did have confidence. It was odd to think that under my unassuming exterior lurked the heart of a gambler. Now that I saw how easy it was, I was actually beginning to enjoy myself. "Did anybody else see that notice about the meeting of the coven?" I asked innocently.

Rob colored. "Look, Amy Rose told me she doesn't have anything to do with witches, Iz. It's got to be somebody's idea of a joke."

Jane twirled a strand of hair around her finger.

"It's not all that funny, though, is it?" She glanced around the table. "What do the rest of you guys think?"

"Dunno," shrugged Carl. "'Madame Eglantine' sounds too prissy to be the head of some kind of weird satanic cult."

"I think they're more pagan," said Melissa. "I think they're like those people that do herbal medicine and talk about the summer solstice and worship the earth. Wiccan I think they're called."

"Do you actually *know* any people like that?" asked Jane.

"Well, I've read about them." Melissa looked suddenly doubtful.

I wanted to ask the others how long the coven had been meeting, but I could see that it had been a mistake to bring it up. Isabel and her friends had discussed it before, which made it a risky subject for me. Furthermore, Rob was obviously touchy about it—maybe because of Amy Rose's rumored involvement.

"So what is Amy Rose really like, Rob?" asked Kaki.

Rob's face froze. "She's okay."

"When is your car supposed to come, Iz?" asked Jane.

"Oh," I glanced at her. "It's already here. I forgot to tell you."

"Boy, I wish I were rich and had a big trust fund," said Kaki.

"I can drop you off at the dealer after school," suggested Jane, "so you can pick it up."

"Maybe you'll let us touch it sometime," sighed Melissa.

Rob stiffened, and I found myself following his gaze. He was looking at a girl whose glossy black hair fell in one thick curl to her shoulder. She was a true brunette with dark, deep-set eyes. The intensity of her gaze gave the impression of fire burning in a cave. Her lips were full and colored with startling red lipstick. She was wearing tight black jeans cinched at the waist by a wide belt with a disklike silver buckle that caught the light and flashed as she moved.

"She sure *looks* like a witch," whispered Kaki.

"Oh, cut it out, you guys," Rob said.

Amy Rose's red lips stretched into an unconvincing smile.

"Don't look at her," Jane told me in a low voice.

But I couldn't look away. Neither could Rob. She was as startling in her way as a total eclipse of the sun. Compared to her, everyone else in the cafeteria was dressed in the equivalent of camouflage. Only Amy Rose stood brazenly before us, not bothering to dress or act like anyone else. The chattering crowd in the cafeteria seemed to grow silent as she passed, as if she were sucking the air out of people's lungs. It was with some surprise that I noticed she was really a small person, probably not more than five feet tall. She made her way to the back of the cafeteria and sat down at a table filled with offbeat-looking kids. As far as I could tell from the distance they seemed to like black T-shirts, combat boots with chains, and ratty hair. Amy Rose was neater and cleaner than the others. Sitting at the head of the table with her commanding expression, she looked like the general of a ragtag army.

I pulled my eyes away from her at last and breathed. "Gee, I wonder what she did on *her* summer vacation."

Rob turned beet red and muttered, "Give me a break, Iz."

Everyone laughed and Rob got even redder. Too late, I realized that it must have sounded as if I were taunting Rob about his summer romance. My fascinated gaze rested on his face. Rob had hooked up with Amy Rose? I simply couldn't imagine it.

CHAPTER 5

I had no trouble finding Jane's car that afternoon. It was parked on the gravel extension to the parking lot, near some fencing that enclosed high-voltage wires. I slid in beside Jane and was startled when she revved up the engine at once and zipped into a line of cars exiting the student parking lot.

"Aren't we going to wait for Rob?" I asked.

Jane looked straight ahead. "He's getting a ride home with Carl. You hurt his feelings, Iz, giving him a hard time about Amy Rose at lunch."

"I didn't mean to," I said truthfully. "I didn't think about how it was going to sound. I just blurted it out."

"The trouble is that you speak first and think

77

later." She smiled wryly. "You know it's true, idiot. You've admitted it yourself."

I should have felt chastened, but instead I felt a flutter of excitement that Isabel and I had shared the same character flaw.

"It was cruel of you to go after him in front of everybody when it's perfectly plain he's trying to make up with you," Jane went on.

"Wait a minute!" I protested. "I didn't force him to get mixed up with Amy Rose. She's not my problem. I'm just surprised he was interested in her, that's all." I thought about it and added, "In fact, I'm astonished."

"Well, you practically drove him into her arms, didn't you? Freezing him out the way you did."

I was surprised at her anger. Shouldn't Jane be trying to see things from Isabel's point of view? Whose friend was she, anyway? I shot her a curious glance. "Are you trying to start a fight with me?"

She looked embarrassed. "Okay, maybe I am a little bit mad at you, Iz. It's like I never know where I am with you anymore."

"I've been through a lot—"

"I mean even before the burglary!" she burst out. "You were acting strange before school was out—you know that. And then you never wrote or called me all summer. Six letters I wrote you, and I only got one back!"

I shot her a startled look.

"Then when I called you up," Jane went on, "you acted so strange, like you didn't even want to hear from me. I told myself that when school started up again I was just going to act like nothing had happened, and see if we could go back to the way we were." Her voice cracked. "But it's hard for me to fake the way I feel. I kept wondering what was going on with you." She fished a tissue out of her purse and blew her nose. "What made you act like that? Are you going to say that you don't want to be friends with me anymore?"

"No!" I said.

"Then what?" she cried.

"I don't know," I said. It looked as if my twin had been foundering in deeper emotional waters than I realized. "I'm sorry," I added inadequately.

Jane wiped her eyes. "I thought maybe you were outgrowing me. Or maybe the stuff with my mother was so depressing that you just didn't want to have anything to do with me anymore. I've been imagining every kind of crazy thing. Then you had that huge fight with Rob, and I thought maybe you were cracking up. I started wondering if there was something going on that you didn't want to tell anybody about, and that's why you were pulling away from us."

"What could be so bad that I wouldn't want to tell you about it?" I wondered aloud.

Jane grinned. "I dunno. When you put it that way, I can see how stupid it sounds. Best friends forever—right?"

"Right." I smiled. The dreadful finality of Isabel's death tore at my heart. Chances were we would never know what had been going on with my unhappy twin, or why she had withdrawn from her friends.

"My mom has really missed you," Jane said softly. "You were always her favorite. You ought to come see her. It's tough for her, not being able to get out."

I squirmed, wishing Isabel were standing offstage giving me cues at these tricky points. I didn't even know what was wrong with Jane's mother.

"I think Mom's worse lately." Jane frowned. "Sometimes she has trouble thinking of words. I don't remember that happening before. Dad says she's pretty much the same, but with him being away all summer working, he hasn't seen the changes the way I have."

"Maybe it's her medication," I ventured. I had once been friends with a girl whose mother was chronically ill, and I remembered her medication had been a constant topic of discussion.

"That's what Dad says." Jane's expression brightened. "He's going to talk to the doctor. I guess I'm getting too focused on little things on account of taking care of her all summer. I felt so guilty about not wanting to be with her. I mean, I know she hates being a burden, and I try to keep telling myself how she took care of me when I was little and she never complained." Jane gave me a guilty glance. "But it's really a relief to get back to school and be around other people, you know?"

"It's okay to want your own life," I said. "She's had hers." That was Liz speaking—Liz, whose mother had dragged her against her will from one strange school to another. Now at last I had wrested the controls into my own hands. It was just that I wasn't quite sure in what direction I was headed.

"It's hard," said Jane, and I saw that her eyes were glistening.

"I know."

She reached for my hand and squeezed it. "Iz, it's so *good* to have you back. I've been so alone." She shot me a dazzling smile as she pulled up to the car dealership. "I hope you won't be too stuck up to speak to the rest of us when you're driving your cool new car."

"Don't worry." I leaped out of the car. A duplicate of Isabel's driver's license was the next thing I'd need, I reflected. It occurred to me that I was behaving as if I intended to go on being Isabel for a while. Smiling, I waved to Jane as she drove away.

Inside the dealership I was jolted when it turned out I had to sign Isabel's name to a receipt for the car. Our signatures were similar but not identical. It was impossible for me to imitate her large, sweeping capital I. My normal writing style was much tidier.

I didn't expect a problem except when signing checks, and I had already decided how I would handle that. I would practice Isabel's signature until I got as close to hers as I could. Then I'd go into the bank and tell them I needed to make out a new signature card because my style of signing had changed. I knew it could be done. Since I had gotten a checkbook younger than most kids, I had already had to change my signature card twice.

The Corvette was the color of a ripe tomato, and I smiled wryly when they drove it out to me. It would draw all eyes wherever it went, that was for sure. I didn't exactly want everyone watching as I tried to get used to driving, but it seemed I didn't have any choice.

When I slid behind the wheel, I felt overcome by the smell of plastic, and I was appalled at how close the car rode to the ground. But I managed to smile at the beaming salesman as I drove out of the lot.

I pulled out onto the highway right behind a big truck. It sprayed diesel exhaust on me when the light changed, and I half-expected to get sucked into its wake as it roared off. I took a deep breath and reminded myself that I was going to have to get used to driving the car sooner or later. I only wished its pointed nose didn't make it so hard for me to guess how close I was to the vehicle ahead of me.

My father's house might not be exactly welcoming, but it was heaven compared to being stuck between two snarling trucks, and I was relieved when at last I pulled up into his driveway. Getting out, I noticed that my palms had left damp marks on the steering wheel.

As soon as I went inside, I saw that the books in the living room had been reshelved, and the carpet showed fresh vacuum marks. The cleaning service had shown up. My father was sitting in an armchair reading, his face gray with exhaustion. "How was school?" he asked.

"Good," I said, smiling at him. Generally I thought of myself as an honest person, and I was surprised that I was having so much fun deceiving everyone. I didn't feel that I was lying. It was more like I had pushed my way through a mirror to find myself in a new world.

My father glanced at me out of the corner of his eye. "How did Isabel's friends take the news?"

I hesitated. "I haven't exactly told them yet."

A peculiar look of satisfaction lit his face. "Quite right," he said. "We don't want a bunch of nosy people paying sympathy calls, do we?"

In a blinding flash I realized that he had expected me all along to step into Isabel's place.

"I got the cleaning people to take your rental car back," he added. "I see that you've already picked up the Corvette."

The idea that my father and I were somehow conspiring in a scheme for me to replace Isabel made me extremely uncomfortable. I had no idea how unbalanced he was, and for the first time it hit me that I might be making a serious mistake. But then Rob's face swam before my eyes. The imprint of his personality had been so strong on my mind that he seemed to fill the room. I knew that in spite of my misgivings I would play this game a little longer.

I turned away. "What's the matter with Jane's mother?" I asked.

"She had a stroke. She can only get around in a wheelchair now, and I believe she must be having some minor strokes as well, or else some unrelated degeneration, because she seems to have lost some of her small motor capacity. She has occasional trouble with choking, and she can't be left alone."

I shot him a sharp glance. "How do you know that if you never go out."

He smiled. "Oh, Isabel was my eyes and ears."

I felt a tingle of relief that he spoke of Isabel in the past tense. Maybe I had been bothered more than I realized by his confusing me with Isabel when I had shown up at the hospital. I was conscious of a desire to put as much distance between him and me as possible. "I think I'll lie down," I said. "It's been a long day."

"I'm sure it has." He smiled at me slyly. He

wore a navy cardigan over a shirt that was open at the throat, revealing tufts of white hair on his thin chest. His pale hands were splayed out over the book that lay on his lap. The fragile, colorless fingers made me think how much like a spider he was.

I fled from him, running up the stairs. As soon as I got to Isabel's room, my eye fell on her chess set. The broken pieces of the shattered rook had been dusted away. I hoped it was the work of the cleaning service. I didn't like to think of my father prowling around my room and pawing through the things in my suitcase.

I stared at the chess set uneasily. A single gemlike stone had been put in place of the piece that had been destroyed. I was like that stone, I thought. I was a marker, keeping Isabel's place. As long as I went through the paces of her normal life, no one had to face the fact that she was dead.

I lay on Isabel's bed, pressing my palms tightly against my temples. Taking Isabel's place was sick. The sensible thing to do was to leave Sewell's Falls tomorrow and fly back to my mother. But I knew I wasn't capable of behaving sensibly. Not now.

I stood up so abruptly that black dots swam before my eyes, and I snatched my twin's yearbook off the bookshelf. Falling onto the bed again, I studied the photographs. I leafed through the book and spotted a number of familiar faces—kids who had spoken to me at school. Inked signatures across some pictures identified other friends.

Whole pages were filled with handwriting. I puzzled over the messages, trying to imagine the personality that had prompted these outpourings of affection. Some people had written about a special feeling of closeness to Isabel; I realized that was not the kind of thing one's close friends wrote. I had already read Jane's contribution, which was so cryptic I couldn't figure it out. That was the way friends spoke to each other, with a lot understood and little spelled out. The other outpourings were the sorts of things people wrote when they weren't good friends but had had long intimate talks. I deduced that Isabel must have been the type people confided in. "A student of the human heart" our father had said. Perhaps she had liked figuring people out. I had a little of that curiosity myself.

I couldn't find a message from Rob—presumably they had broken up by the time the yearbooks came out—but on the back leaf some boy had written lyrically of the first time he had seen Isabel. I couldn't make out his scrawled signature. Flipping over a few pages, I came to another handful of lines that read almost the same way, but this boy's spelling was terrible. What the two passages had in common was their breathless focus on Isabel.

I lifted my head and stared at the image I could see reflected in the mirror through the open bathroom door. No one had written messages like that in my yearbook. I had hesitated about even buying a yearbook at the last school I attended, and I was embarrassed to remember how few people had signed it. Only scant and empty, polite comments about what fun we'd had in English class were in my book. A lump grew in my throat when I thought of all I had missed in my roving life.

I pulled a scratch pad out of my purse and wrote "Isabel Herrick." Not bad. It could have passed as the real thing. I got Isabel's letter from my suitcase, stared at the signature, then tried it again several times. Practice makes perfect.

Isabel must have had all the confidence that comes from belonging, and I envied that. But I had my own kind of confidence from kicking around in odd corners of the world. I knew I could cope with whatever came along. And that was exactly the sort of self-confidence I needed for this adventure.

The phone rang and I jumped for it. "Hello?"

"Hi, Iz. It's Rob."

I sucked in my breath. It seemed important that I get one thing cleared up right away. "Rob, I wasn't trying to get at you about Amy Rose. I was just startled when I saw her, that's all. I wasn't thinking. I guess it was hard for me to imagine you two together."

"She's just an ordinary person," he said stiffly.

"Oh, I'm sure," I said, though I didn't believe it for a minute.

"Are you mad at me?" he asked.

"No!" I protested.

"You don't sound like yourself."

"I can't help it, but I'm not mad."

"Cross your heart and hope to die?"

I could hear the catch in his voice and my heart sank. There was some special way Isabel was supposed to respond to that, and I didn't know what it was.

"Uh-huh," I mumbled.

"What's wrong?" he said sharply. "Are you okay, Iz?"

"I'm fine!" I cried. "I just I have a lot on my mind."

"Why don't you try telling me what's on your

mind for a change?"

I choked and drew a blank.

"I see you're not exactly rushing to share," he went on with some bitterness.

"It's—it's not that I'm hiding anything," I stuttered. "It's only that I'm so shaken up by the burglary. They broke into this house, too. I don't think I mentioned that. I guess they used my keys to get in, because when Dad and I got back here somebody had ransacked the place. It was scary. We had to have all the locks in the house changed."

"Did you call the cops?"

"Of course!" I said sharply. "What makes you think we wouldn't have called the cops?"

"I dunno," he said slowly. "Sometimes I feel as if I hardly know you anymore."

A long silence fell. I was listening to my heartbeat. This was my chance to tell Rob the truth, I realized. But I knew now that I couldn't.

"When you took off for the beach, I figured it was all over between us," he went on. "You were acting like you never wanted to see me again, but I kept thinking about you, anyway. Maybe I'm not making any sense."

"No, I understand. You had unfinished business," I said. "I've had that feeling, too." But my unfinished business was Isabel's murder.

"Now I look at you and it's almost like looking at a stranger," Rob said. "Even the way you talk to me seems different."

My heart stopped. I thought I had been pulling off the impersonation perfectly, but Rob was telling me that he sensed something different.

"You've changed," he said.

I shrank into myself, feeling like a cheap imitation. But at the same time I could feel defiance surging in me. Rob could never prove that I wasn't Isabel. After a while he would forget the way she had talked. New memories overlay old ones quickly—no one knew that better than I, who had picked up stakes and moved again and again. "People grow up," I said. "Everybody changes."

"Are you trying to tell me something?" he asked.

"Like what?" My voice sounded tentative even to my own ears.

"I don't know. I thought maybe you were starting to say that you were getting steadier. Something like that."

Wishful thinking. I recognized his tone now. I had heard it often enough in my own voice. *Maybe this is the man Mom will decide to marry. Maybe this is the place we'll stay for good.* From what Rob was saying, I guessed that Isabel must have had a problem focusing on one boy. "Maybe we should just let the past go and enjoy the present," I said.

"Does this mean you're going to stop giving me a hard time about Amy Rose?" Rob asked.

"I'll try," I said.

"And I guess I'm not supposed to ask any questions about the guy on the motorcycle?" he asked.

What guy on a motorcycle? Did Isabel have more little surprises to spring on me? "He's history," I said, choking a little.

"This is crazy, Iz," Rob said. "You complicate my life, you drive me crazy, I can never figure out what you're thinking, half the time I'm *afraid* to know what you're thinking, and somehow I can't stay away from you. What do you think that means?"

"We're attracted to one another?" I ventured.

He laughed. "My mom is calling me. I've got to go. Can I call you back after dinner?"

"Better not," I said. "I've got a lot to do." I glanced at the scratch pad on the bed with four reasonably good versions of Isabel's signature.

"Are you sure this doesn't have anything to do

with the guy on the motorcycle?" he said.

"I can't believe you said that!" I cried indignantly.

"I can't believe I did either. I'm sorry. We'll start over, okay?"

"We'll be friends," I said with all the firmness I could muster.

"Friends."

"See you tomorrow."

"Sure."

I hung up with my ears tingling. If a motorcycle roared up outside I was going to scream, that's all. I was going to tell whoever drove up on the front lawn that Isabel was dead. One of Isabel's old boyfriends at a time was all I could cope with.

I sat on the bed, propped the yearbook against my knees, and stared at it intently. On the next page I was brought up short when I found myself gazing at Isabel's picture. It should have been the face I saw in the mirror, but it wasn't. It took me a few minutes to figure out what was wrong.

Isabel and I were "mirror twins," Mother had explained to me once. The cowlick curl that was at my left temple was at Isabel's right. That meant that Isabel looked exactly like my image in the mirror because a mirror reverses the sides of the image. Photographs don't. The picture in the yearbook had been printed wrong because the printers had inadvertently reversed the negative. I smiled. So much the better. If Rob noticed my cowlick was on the wrong side and checked the yearbook picture, he would decide his memory was wrong.

Fate was making it easy for me at every step, giving me lots of green lights. It didn't occur to me then that there was any danger in going with those green lights.

I went downstairs and fixed myself something to eat. Dusk was gathering under the trees, and I had to strain my eyes to see the white timbers and oriental-style roof of the gazebo. What had possessed my father to build such an impractical structure out in the woods? Maybe Isabel had used the gazebo for romantic trysts with guys on motorcycles. I didn't think she would have brought a boy dressed in black leather to the house.

Tomorrow, I decided, I would take a look at the gazebo.

CHAPTER

6

I sat up suddenly in bed, cold with fear. When a sharp electronic buzz sounded in my ear, I realized what had woken me. It was the sound I had heard in my sleep the night before. I leaped out of bed. As the soles of my bare feet hit the floor, I heard the buzz again. Then silence.

I stood beside the bed. The sound had been so directionless, I wasn't sure I could have traced it even if it was still buzzing. *The alarm must be hidden someplace close to my bed. But why would Isabel have set an alarm to go off in the middle of the night?*

The curtains of the room were open and I saw that a light was moving outside. Pressing my forehead against the cold windowpane, I peered into the darkness. The light stopped moving and glowed brightly from behind the trees. Someone was at the gazebo! I felt dangerously visible and stepped away from the window.

Shadows moved in my empty bedroom. I realized that the bright light in the woods must be throwing moving shadows into my window. Standing a few paces from the window, I watched as the light halted. What if the biker had come for Isabel? My heart jumped into my throat as I pictured a biker in black leather creeping through the trees. I gripped my own arms tightly, trying to stop my trembling. *Whoa,* I thought, my teeth chattering. *If the biker killed Isabel, then he would know she was dead and wouldn't be coming to the gazebo to meet her. Right?* But reason couldn't quiet my heart.

Straining, I could hear a faint noise in the distance. Not music. Voices perhaps. I could see that the light was not the faintly yellowish one given off by a headlight or the weak beam of a flashlight. It was like the white glare cast by the gasoline lantern people used when they went camping.

For a long time I stared out the window. The light illuminated the gazebo so that its white timbers showed through the trees. I made out moving shadows. Slowly I realized that the shadows in my room had begun to shift. That meant the light must be moving. A few minutes later the woods went dark, and I heard the low rumble of engines.

My flesh felt cold as I crawled back under my sheets. I glanced at the luminous dial of my watch. The meeting of the coven, I remembered, had been set for 2 A.M. Wednesday. That was now. Today!

Before I left for school the next morning, I plucked a long blond hair from my head and, standing on tiptoe, laid it at the top of my bedroom door. Then I carefully closed the door so the fine hair was trapped up there. If my father was creeping into my room while I was gone, I would know.

The Corvette drew stares as I drove into the school parking lot. As Jane had predicted, gravel pinged against its shiny finish. I felt annoyed at Isabel for buying a car that would force me to get up earlier in order to get a decent parking place.

"Cool car!" someone called out.

"Wow!"

Kids yelled good-natured compliments at me

when I got out, and I had to force myself to erase my frown and wave at them. "Some car!" Rob called.

I turned around and smiled in relief as I watched him unfold his long legs from an Oldsmobile that was covered with the scratches and dents of venerable age.

"I'm having second thoughts," I said ruefully. "Do I really want my car to get more compliments than me?"

Rob walked over to me and put his arm around me. "I didn't know you ever had second thoughts, Iz."

He was looking at me with such an unwavering gaze, it took a strong effort of will not to raise my hand and self-consciously touch my cowlick.

His hand rested lightly at my hip, and I realized that I hadn't even questioned the possessiveness of his gesture. Now I looked into his hazel eyes and found my breath coming fast. The kids around the parking lot had mysteriously stopped calling out to me. Or maybe I had only quit hearing them. It was as if a curtain had dropped around the two of us, sealing us in a private world.

"When we said last night that we were going to be friends," Rob said in a low voice, "does that mean I don't get to touch you?"

I swallowed. "No."

"Good." He brushed his lips lightly against my cheek.

I knew suddenly that I wanted very much for him to kiss me. My sensible decision to keep the relationship between us on a friendly footing had faded away. It was as if I had lost my balance and some unexpected momentum was carrying me forward.

We linked hands, and gravel crunched under our feet as we walked toward the buildings. *Okay,* I told myself. *So maybe we were a little more than friends. What's the harm in it?* We had to let go of each other's hands to thread our way through the parked cars of the big parking lot. I stepped out of the line of cars too quickly and Rob pulled me sharply out of the path of a speeding Chevy. He held me close to him for a full minute. "How can it feel so good to be with you," Rob said in a low voice, "when we fight all the time?"

I looked up at him. "I don't want to fight with you. I can't think of anything we would want to fight about."

Rob took my hand in his and lifted my fingers one by one, ticking off reasons. "You go out with other guys, and you lie to me about it. You're too busy to see me, but you're mad if I don't drop everything to see you. You try to change the way I am." He lifted my other hand. "On the other hand," he smiled, "I criticize your dad. I don't want to go out on school nights. I don't have your sense of humor, and I can't afford to go with you to fancy restaurants. Hey, wait a minute. I'm running out of hands and I still haven't run out of the reasons we fight." I noticed that his smile did not reach his eyes. "At least we're used to it, right?" he said.

The picture he had painted was dark, and suddenly I was having trouble getting my breath. *This is not my life,* I reminded myself. *I can walk away from it.* But I knew that every minute I was with Rob made it harder to face telling him the truth. "I get the feeling you don't really want to be . . . friends," I said.

"I can't help it," he said promptly. "You're like a bad habit."

"I don't want to be your bad habit." Without meaning to, I fingered my cowlick uneasily.

"Then I guess we ought not to see each other anymore," he said. But even as he was saying it, he drew me closer.

I looked up into his eyes and reminded myself

firmly that I wasn't Isabel. It was Isabel Rob cared about. But just the same, my knees felt strangely weak.

"You know I hate fighting with you," he said. "It's just—"

"Just what?" I said quickly.

"I don't want you to go out with other guys. I can't help it. And I can't pretend that your father is perfect either. That's the way it is—I can't change, you can't change. It's a mess."

"I can change."

"Yeah." He grinned. "What are we talking about here—a brain transplant?"

"We are talking about being friends who trust each other. That's what I thought, anyway."

He frowned. "Are you okay, Iz? You just don't sound—"

"Like myself?" I finished.

He nodded, looking puzzled.

"Maybe I'm growing up."

We walked on in silence, stepped up on the curb, and followed the sidewalk to the main building. What Rob had said bothered me. I had to remind myself that I hadn't heard Isabel's side, and that the entire relationship might look different from her point of view. It could be that

Rob was paranoid and insanely jealous. Or maybe his idea of eating cheap was sharing a bag of corn chips in the parking lot. There were any number of possibilities.

I really needed to make delicate inquiries of Jane about what had gone on between Rob and Isabel, but that was out of the question. It was ironic that my chief purpose was to find out about Isabel, yet I was cut off from asking any questions because people thought *I* was Isabel. The total insanity of what I was doing swept over me and made me catch my breath in dismay.

The bell rang and Rob said, "See you at lunch." He grinned and plunged into the shuffling bunch of kids surging toward their classrooms, leaving me alone on the walkway.

I couldn't move for a minute. A panic attack, I guess. But after a while I realized I was staring at the school bulletin board. The small notice about the meeting of the coven had disappeared and only a thumbtack hole in the cork showed me where it had been. Could Isabel have been a member of the coven? That would explain why she had set her alarm for 2 A.M. But I had the idea she had accused Amy Rose of being in the coven, which seemed odd if she had been mixed up in it herself.

"Hey, Iz," said a boy with long flaxen hair. "How's it going?"

"Great!" I switched on my smile. I had lost count of how many times kids had spoken to me. It felt like I was running for public office.

I had never understood why some had the charisma or warmth or whatever it was that drew people to them and others didn't, even though, as a lonely observer, I had had plenty of time to think about it. The X quality seemed to be more than a sum of the obvious advantages of beauty and self-confidence. It was a kind of incandescence. When people had it, nothing else mattered. And it looked as if Isabel had had it.

At lunch later that day, our table buzzed with chatter, but I didn't have much to say. It didn't help that Rob hardly took his eyes off of me the whole time. Maybe he had noticed the little curl at my temple. Or maybe he was onto something I hadn't even thought of yet. My stomach was in knots. Somehow my game had taken on a desperate quality. Perhaps it was because for the first time I had begun to care whether or not I got found out.

CHAPTER 7

That afternoon, when I slid into the Corvette, I spotted a package lying on the seat beside me, wrapped in shiny white paper and tied with a bow. Ripping it open, I saw a tangle of green leaves and something shiny. I realized that I was looking at a boy's large class ring almost obscured by a leafy swatch of greenery. Nestled among the leaves was an artificial pink flower that looked like a wild rose. I tried to disentangle the ring, but when I tugged at it I felt a sharp stab of pain. A closer look showed wicked thorns on the rose; even the undersides of the leaves had hair-thin barbs. Hastily I dropped the tangled leaves back into the box.

It was a miracle I didn't hit someone as I sped out of the parking lot. I know I was frightened. I could feel the pins and needles of unused adrenaline in my feet. I hadn't driven very far when I realized that the flesh was tight across my cheekbones and my eyes ached. The car began to weave. Panicked, I pulled off the road and guided the car behind a strip of stores in a small shopping center where cardboard boxes littered the uneven pavement and weeds struggled up through the cracks in the asphalt. Feeling sick, I leaned my head against the steering wheel. I rolled the window down and gasped for air. *Poison,* I thought. A gritty breeze swept into the car and fluttered the discarded wrapping paper on the seat beside me.

A blur of gray streaked before my eyes, and I heard a thump. A cat had landed on the hood of the car with a snarl, and I yelped in surprise. It leaped off and I watched its black rump disappear into the underbrush. Dusty paw marks on the car's shining hood showed where it had briefly perched.

With a vague sense of surprise, I realized that I felt normal again. During the brief instant that I had been too startled to think about poison, I had been breathing fine. It looked as if the only poison acting on me was the poison of my powerful imagination. I remembered now that I hadn't eaten lunch, which probably explained the dizziness.

The sky was darkening as a storm gathered in the west, and I shivered. Even if no poison had been on the thorns, there had been malice in the gift.

I suppose I drove too fast getting back to the house. It didn't seem to matter. In my present state of mind, I couldn't believe that I would die in an ordinary traffic accident. The phone was ringing when I opened the front door, and I ran into the kitchen and snatched it up.

"Hello?"

"Hi. This is Amy Rose."

"Amy Rose?" I replied cautiously.

"I think you remember who I am." She laughed.

An uneasy silence fell. Finally I asked, "What do you want?"

"I just wondered how you're *feeling*."

I heard laughter and then a click as the line went dead.

"Was that *Rob*?" My father's sarcastic voice startled me. I stepped out into the dining room and faced him.

"No, it was a girl from school," I said. My father made me feel transparent, as if he were able to see the thoughts in my head. I suppose the malicious package had undermined my confidence. Up till now I had been the only actor in a purely personal drama. Now I had been put on notice that Amy Rose was making a move. I didn't like it.

I grabbed my books off the couch and ran upstairs. The single golden hair was still an almost invisible glimmer at the top of the door. My father hadn't been in my room, at least.

I went in and rummaged through Isabel's drawers until I found a pair of gloves. They were leather, good protection against thorns. I ran downstairs. To my relief, my father had disappeared and I was able to get the package from my car without any of his acid remarks.

Once back in my room I put the gloves on and was able to pull the ring free of its tangle of thorns. I tucked the gloves in my back pocket. Turning the ring over in my bare palm, I could read the initials engraved inside it—R. O. B.

The phone by the bed rang and I picked it up. "Hello?" I listened carefully for a click, for any sign that my father had picked up on the extension. The call from Amy Rose had made me paranoid.

"Iz? It's Rob."

I stared at the ring in my hand. "Rob, I've got

something of yours. A ring with initials engraved inside it—R. O. B. That's yours, isn't it?"

"I didn't give it to her, Iz," he said. "She just took it. What was I going to do, file a report with the police? I'd look pretty stupid." He added, after a moment, "You can keep it if you want."

"What does the O stand for?"

"You know! Oscar. After my grandfather Oscar—lucky me."

"Oh, right. I forgot."

"Are you okay? You aren't having headaches or anything are you?"

"No, I'm fine."

"You do believe me, don't you, Iz? Amy Rose just took it."

"Of course I believe you," I said. When I glanced out the open window, I could make out the peaked roof of the gazebo. "I've got to go, Rob. There's something I have to do."

"You aren't trying to get rid of me, are you?"

"You know better than that." I smiled.

"It's really good to hear you sounding like yourself again."

"Of course I'm myself," I said, freezing suddenly. Who was I was trying to reassure? Rob or me? The eerie ease with which I had stepped into Isabel's place made me feel as if I was losing track of who I was. Little mistakes at least reassured me that I was still Liz inside. It was like plucking cards blindly from a deck, I realized. In some strange way I felt better when I picked the wrong card.

After I had hung up, I went outside and made my way through the woods to the gazebo. I had Isabel's green gloves tucked in my hip pocket, partly because of the irrational feeling that they were a good luck talisman and would keep me safe. Dry leaves crackled under my feet as I crept through the woods. The sky was dark overhead, and a fresh breeze stirred the pines. Loose pine needles slithered into my shoes and pricked my feet. A squirrel scolded me from the treetops.

When I reached the gazebo, my shoes sank into soft dirt and I smelled something like cilantro. Glancing down I saw that my heel had crushed a plant in what looked like an herb garden.

I climbed the steps and glanced around at the sturdy beams on which the roof rested, each ornately grooved in the Chippendale style. A border had been amateurishly painted along the edge of the floor and was captioned with the names of plants—rosemary, thyme, nettle, eglantine. Eglantine?

Several white chalk circles overlapped each other on the floor of the pentagon-shaped structure. I remembered hearing that magic spells always begin with the magician drawing a new circle, and I knew I had found the meeting place of the coven.

Then I heard the sound of a car. A through road was not far, and I told myself the sound of a passing car meant nothing. But I couldn't stop myself from glancing around anxiously. I leaped off the platform and landed in the soft dirt of the herb garden. All my instincts told me to get out of there, and I hurried back to the house.

"What are you doing with Isabel's gloves?" my father said sharply when I stepped indoors.

"I'm using them." I could hear my voice rising shrilly. "Do you have a problem with that?"

He took a quick step backward, and I saw his Adam's apple bob convulsively. "Of course, you may take whatever you like." But it was obvious that, in spite of his words, the thought of my claiming Isabel's belongings filled him with panic. I wanted to shake him hard and remind him that I was his daughter, too.

Ignoring him, I pulled a heavy dictionary off the bookshelf and laid it down on the coffee table. I looked up "eglantine." A kind of old rose. A rose. Amy Rose. Amy Rose had to be Mme. Eglantine. She wasn't even making any secret of it. After all, she had left the rose as a calling card in the sinister little package. I wondered how much Isabel had known about Amy Rose's activities at the gazebo.

"Did Isabel keep a diary?" I asked.

"Yes, of course," he said stiffly. "A diary is the perfect practice for a budding writer."

"I can't find it," I said. "In fact, except for a bundle of canceled checks in the desk drawer, I can't find anything with Isabel's handwriting on it." It had occurred to me that without any copy of Isabel's handwriting, it would be difficult for anyone to prove that I *wasn't* Isabel.

"Isabel had been trying to eliminate paper from her life." My father's mouth closed into a tight line.

"You're telling me she kept her diary on a computer? Of course," I said slowly. "I should have thought of that." Isabel had loved games, I remembered, and a computer was the obvious toy for the modern game freak.

"Not on her desktop computer," he added. "She had a pocket computer no bigger than a small notebook. The Wiz, she called it. It combined several functions that I never quite got straight—alarm clock, diary, appointment calendar. I believe it also had an infrared beam that would allow it to communicate with other similar units. I gave it to her for Christmas."

That must be what the buzz was—the alarm function of Isabel's tiny computer. That meant it must be hidden somewhere in her room. But why didn't she take the little computer with her to the beach for the summer? Either she must have decided to quit keeping a diary, or she had written something in it that she needed to hide.

"Where did Isabel keep it?" I asked.

"On her desk, I suppose. I never noticed particularly." He shrugged. "I expect it's gone now. Taken by thieves."

I decided not to mention the alarm that went off in my room every night. I had already seen how possessive my father was about Isabel's gloves. I wouldn't have put it past him to try to confiscate Isabel's diary if I found it.

CHAPTER 8

The storm broke during the night. Hovering uneasily between sleep and waking, I felt thunder shake the house and heard the rain hit spitefully against my window. Suddenly the hidden buzzer sounded, jolting me wide awake. I sprang out of bed, hitting my knee against the desk in my hurry. I rubbed my injured knee and hopped around swearing, but it was no use. The buzzing had already stopped.

Morning dawned damp and drizzly. Gloom had set in for the day, and I had a headache. But I had made a decision. Trying to find the missing computer at night was hopeless. I would have to do a thorough search during the daytime. It was a shame that the hidden computer was so small. It could be anywhere, even under floorboards or baseboards.

My "Isabel smile" was on automatic pilot as I found my way to class that morning. I was so tired I felt as if I were sleepwalking. When I got to homeroom, I fell into the chair at my desk and stared out the window at the gloom outside. The radiator below the classroom window was leprous with peeling paint, and I could hear the pop and crack of someone chewing gum behind me.

"Isabel?" The voice seemed far away. "Isabel Herrick," Mrs. Willard repeated sharply.

I jumped and stared at her. I always responded instinctively to "Iz." It sounded so much like my own name that it caught my attention. In my present state of stupefied fatigue, Isabel's full name hadn't penetrated.

"You have an appointment with the school counselor to talk about college," Mrs. Willard said. "You're on today's list, so you'd better check your schedule."

I hadn't even glanced at my course schedule since the first day of school. I flipped my notebook open to where I had clipped it to the inside cover. Typed at the bottom of the sheet was today's date with the notation, "College counseling appointment —Mr. Crumpler, 8:45."

"You'd better get over to the office right away," said Mrs. Willard. "Those appointments are tightly scheduled, and if you're late you might miss yours." I noticed that most of my classmates, upon being reminded of their own appointments, looked as bewildered as I felt. No one seemed ready to think about college.

As I made my way through the open passageways, the wet air made my clothes feel clammy. I kept my eyes down as I trotted to the office. The Isabel smile was more than I could manage right now. Crumpled notebook paper, candy wrappers, and dead leaves had gathered in damp corners, and tiny weeds struggled to grow in the cracks in the sidewalk. *Step on a crack, break your mother's back.* My mother was probably sunning herself on a ship in the Mediterranean about now. I knew what she would think of what I was doing. "Liz, are you out of your mind?" Her lilting voice sounded in my brain like a mockingbird's cry.

When I got to the office, I saw a bunch of confused-looking kids standing in the waiting room awaiting their turns. The boy with the white frizzy hair perked up when he saw me. "Hi, Iz," he said. "Can you believe they're talking to us about college? Man, I'm not ready."

115

"Me either," I said.

Six disbelieving pair of eyes were turned on me like searchlights, and I could feel my face getting warm. "Where are you guys going to apply?" I asked before they could notice that I didn't have Isabel's poise.

"Anywhere that'll take me, I guess," said the kid with the white hair.

The secretary called my name, and with some relief I left the others waiting in the front office. It was easier to deal with adults. No charisma was needed or expected. All I had to do was be polite.

I followed the secretary down a short hall to a door marked CRUMPLER. Mr. Crumpler must be Jane's father. That explained why Jane hadn't been able to start a petition about seniors' parking—her father worked at the school. I had been too fixed on my own concerns to bother putting the pieces together before now.

When I pushed the door open, I saw Mr. Crumpler was on the phone. His swivel chair was turned to the side so that he was silhouetted against the blinds, which made his profile look faintly scalloped. He was a big man with wavy chestnut-brown hair.

I took my seat so quietly, I was afraid he might

not have noticed that I had arrived. I decided I'd better say something so he would know I was there. "I'm here for my appointment," I murmured.

The phone receiver clattered on the desk as Mr. Crumpler spun around to face me. He looked so pale I was afraid he must have just gotten bad news. I remembered that Jane's mother was gravely ill and that he had been scheduled to talk to the doctor.

"Is everything all right?" I asked.

He groped blindly for the fallen phone receiver. "Yes. I'm sorry. You startled me." He spoke into the receiver. "I'll call you back," he said briefly. The receiver clicked as he dropped it back into place.

"I'm sorry to hear," I began, "that things are going so badly with—" It suddenly hit me that I had no idea what Isabel called Mrs. Crumpler. "—your wife," I finished triumphantly. "Jane told me it's been a rough summer."

He was very pale. "Yes." He fiddled with papers on his desk. "Yes, it's been very rough. Particularly on Jane. But we've been lucky enough to get a good woman to look after Nell, and that's all we can ask for right now." His eyes were dark pools of pain. Hard as it had been for me to deal with Isabel's death, I realized that it would be infinitely harder to watch someone I love die inch by inch. Already I was feeling guilty that I had not yet made a point of visiting Jane's mother. "And how was your summer?" Mr. Crumpler asked in a strained voice, eerily echoing my own feeble conversational gambit.

It was pretty obvious he didn't want to talk about his wife's illness, so I went along with his desire to change the subject. "I guess Jane told you about our burglary at the beach," I said.

"No." He blinked. "I got in rather late last night. I've been away at a workshop."

"I got a pretty bad head injury during the break-in, so there are parts of the summer I don't even remember." I was vague about Isabel's academic history and didn't want him to ask me about her course work, so I added cautiously, "A few things seem to be missing from my memory."

"What does the doctor say?" Mr. Crumpler fiddled with his pen.

I shrugged. "It's no big deal. The memories could come back today, tomorrow, or never. But it's not as if there's any real brain damage. I'm okay."

Mr. Crumpler pulled a folder out of a filing

cabinet. He moved mechanically, like a man who had done the same thing hundreds of times. I suppose he had. "So what sort of college do you have in mind?" he asked. "Or have you gotten that far?"

"One in the northeast, I suppose. I'd like not to be too far away from my grandparents." I was able to tell him the list of schools that Isabel and I had settled on. As I spoke I felt a pang knowing that Isabel and I could never meet at college now.

"It looks like you have everything well in hand." He smiled. "No counseling needed here. On to the next student."

I stood up to go. "What do you know about Amy Rose?" I asked impulsively.

"I'm sorry, I can't discuss another student with you," he said.

Mr. Crumpler plucked pamphlets from some stacks on his desk—*The Private College Option; Women's Colleges: Pros and Cons; A Student's Guide to Financial Aid.* He smiled a little and replaced the financial-aid pamphlet. "I don't suppose you'll be needing that," he remarked.

"No," I agreed. "Grandmother Hilliard has pretty much taken care of the money angle." I tucked the pamphlets into my notebook.

"I shouldn't say this," he said, "but if I were you, I'd keep my distance from Amy Rose. From what I hear, she's deeply into some sort of cult, and she has a lot of power over less strong-minded girls."

"Are you trying to tell me that she's dangerous?"

"I can't say that," he said. "Just be careful."

My eye was drawn to the neat bandage on my finger, and I felt an odd squeeze in my stomach that I supposed was fear.

CHAPTER 9

When I got home from school that afternoon, there was no sign of my father. A letter lay on the coffee table with a foreign stamp. It was in my mother's handwriting and addressed to me—Liz Herrick. I stared at the address a full minute, feeling unmasked.

Then I took it upstairs to my room, noticing as I went in that the single blond hair I had laid on the door was still in its place. Leaving it there each morning had become a habit with me. And each afternoon I felt a peculiar satisfaction in assuring myself that my father had not gone into my room while I was away.

I tore open the letter, trying to remember when she had last written me. Telephoning was more her style. Probably she had been driven to write only because she was afraid my father would pick up the phone. Her handwriting seemed to dance merrily over the page. She had never gotten the knack of making all her letters slant in the same direction.

Dearest Liz,

I cannot believe that *even your father* would read your private mail, but do check and see if this envelope has been steamed open and resealed and, of course, write to let me know if it arrives safely. Not that I really think he would destroy your mail, but still—let me know. I am utterly sick with worry. Please, please, please write or phone and let me know how you are getting along. I have scarcely slept a wink since you set off.

Of course, I remind myself that you are not *his* daughter—not in any but the strictly technical sense. You are mine, and I know I can count on your being sensible as you always have been.

But call, write, communicate, darling! I am so worried!

My dearest love,
Mom

A string of addresses, phone numbers, and fax numbers followed her signature. I would have to write her. I was afraid that if I phoned, I might give too much away just by my tone of voice.

Now that I had met my father, it was hard for me to figure out what had brought my parents together. It must have been one of the most flagrant examples on record of opposites attracting. *Time the Magician*, the title of my father's most famous book, seemed in retrospect like a bitter prediction. Once my father had been young and famous, and had some quality that could attract a rich, pretty, frivolous woman. But then he had curdled. Looking at him, it was hard for me to believe he had ever been young.

I heaped my hair on top of my head and checked the effect in the bathroom mirror. Rob was picking me up in a couple of hours for dinner. It was funny how much more attractive I felt since I had stepped into Isabel's life.

I sat down at the desk and wrote to my mother. It felt odd to be using the very writing paper that Isabel had used in her letters to me.

Dear Mom,
    Dad is fully as weird as you said, but

don't worry—I don't see much of him. He hardly ever comes out of his room, except to fix himself a sandwich, and as far as I can tell he eats practically nothing. He's very thin, and whenever I go into his room to check on him, I have the sensation he is going to turn transparent and disappear. He looks terrible. I suppose he's sinking under his grief over Isabel's death.

I'm having fun at school, have met some nice people, and am learning about my twin and meeting her friends, which is interesting. In short—no problems. Enjoy the sun.

Love,
Liz

I remembered Mom's suspicion that my father steamed envelopes open. It wasn't like her to be so paranoid, and I started wondering if she had some good reason to think my father snooped in other people's mail. I didn't really think he would try to read the letter I had written to Mom. But why take the chance? When I had stamped and sealed the letter, I stuffed it in my pocketbook.

I ran downstairs and knocked on my father's bedroom door. "Go away," he said.

Ignoring that, I pushed open the door and went in. He was in bed in his pajamas, with a book facedown on his stomach. Hearing me come in, he lifted it and pretended to read, but I noticed that he was holding it upside down. His lips trembled.

"You don't look good," I said. "Hadn't I'd better call the doctor?"

The deep creases that bracketed his thin mouth curved suddenly, and he smiled as he turned his head to look at me. "You're afraid I'm going to die before I can tell you everything you want to know about Isabel, aren't you?"

That was close enough to the truth to make me uncomfortable. "Don't worry," he said hoarsely. "I'll tell you everything that you need to know. The important thing is that Isabel be kept safe."

I stared at him. "Isabel is dead," I said.

"Of course." His mouth snapped shut. "Sometimes I get confused."

I wondered how much of my father's condition was due to his shock at losing Isabel. If grief was killing him, a doctor might not be able to do him any good, so what was the point of forcing one on him? I shrugged. "I'm going out in a while," I said.

"With Rob?" he asked quickly.

I didn't answer his question. "If you want

anything, I can get it for you before I go," I said.

"You are going out with Rob, aren't you?" His eyes glittered. "Do you *like* him?"

I backed out and closed his bedroom door quietly, but my heart was racing. I knew he was angry at Rob for daring to go out with Isabel. That was why he was so indecently gleeful that Rob had been tricked into going out with me instead. It was sick.

The glitter in my father's eyes haunted me as I made my way back to my room. I ran upstairs, shut the door to my bedroom, and searched frantically for Isabel's diary. The desperation of my search surprised me. I wondered what I was hoping to find. Details about Isabel's romance with Rob? Or maybe some sort of implicit permission to do what I was doing?

I dragged every book off the shelf and checked to make sure none had been hollowed out to conceal a small computer. Then I pulled stuffed animals down from the top shelf of the closet and squeezed each one to make sure nothing had been hidden inside. I unzipped purses and probed the pockets of Isabel's jackets. It was while I was eyeing the bed's mattress that it struck me. I was doing exactly what the intruder had done, going over the same territory. I recalled he had slashed

Isabel's mattress as if he thought something might be hidden in it. Had he been looking for Isabel's diary? But why? It made no sense.

Glancing at my watch, I was alarmed to see that I barely had time to get dressed for dinner. I pulled the closet open. Isabel had a lot of clothes, and the hangers were tightly packed. When I first had the impulse to step into Isabel's place, it had seemed as if I were trying to get close to her. But now I sometimes had the sensation that I was stealing her life. I wanted so many things that she had. Security. Popularity. Rob. And I was helping myself, wasn't I?

I caught my breath sharply. It was crazy to think I was hurting Isabel by what I was doing, I reminded myself. She was dead. But when I pulled out a sweater, I noticed that my movements were jerky.

When I came downstairs, Dad was sitting in the living room. I thought I knew why he had gone to the trouble of dragging himself out of bed. He wanted to see for himself whether Rob came to the door. "You're wearing Isabel's favorite sweater," he observed.

"Are you telling me I ought not to wear it?" I demanded.

"No." He smiled and let his head fall back against the back of the chair. "Wear it. Go ahead."

I could see traces of the strong man he had once been in the broadness of his shoulders and the blunt lines of his face, but try as I might I could not feel that I was related to him. Mom had been right—he was my father only in a technical sense.

The doorbell rang, signaling my chance for escape. I flung the door open.

"It *is* Rob." My father sighed with satisfaction, sinking deeper into the cushions.

Rob nodded. "Evening, sir. Ready, Iz?"

I went outside, locking the door behind me with a firm twist of the key.

"Your father looks awful!" Rob said. "I guess you must be worried sick about him, huh?"

"No," I said tightly. "I'm not. Believe me, he's a lot tougher than he looks."

Rob shot me a curious look. "Did you two have a fight or something?" he asked.

I didn't trust myself to speak, so I simply shook my head and climbed into his old car. Its upholstery was ripped and it smelled of dogs, but I felt myself relax as I sank into it.

"What do you hear from the police about your stolen car?" asked Rob, getting in.

I shook my head. "Nothing."

"Maybe one of those gangs that cut cars up for parts got hold of it. We don't usually get that down here, but I guess anything's possible."

"It doesn't matter. I've got another car now." *What I don't have,* I thought, *is a sister.* I felt a painful ache of grief in my throat. Isabel was gone and had left me alone with my father. It was like a dark fairy tale—a gnome steals a beautiful girl and leaves a malicious old man in her place.

"The summer at the beach must have done you good," Rob said as he backed out of the driveway.

"Why do you keep saying things like that?" I twisted a strand of my hair. "Talking about how I've changed and all."

"I don't know," he said. We had stopped at a light and he looked at me closely, his eyes seeming to bore into me while I squirmed inside. "It's a lot of little things, I guess," he went on. "Like lately you seem to hear what I say when I talk to you. Before you went away I had the feeling you were only half there."

"I guess I was working out some things."

"Everything okay, now?" He touched my arm gently.

"You know better than that. Nothing is ever

perfect. There's always a worm in the apple." In a quick, impatient gesture, I lifted my hair and let it fall behind the seat.

Rob smiled. "You seem happier, anyway."

"I guess I am," I admitted. Nobody would describe my position as easy. But at least it was intensely interesting. And I *was* happier.

My vague answer seemed to satisfy Rob. It was plain that he was used to getting evasions from Isabel. No matter how infuriatingly vague I got, he never tried to dig a straight answer out of me. It was convenient, of course.

He smiled. "Welcome home, Iz." The way he said it made the words so achingly intimate that I fell silent.

We drove through the dark streets, splashing through the water that stood at the edges of the road. Traffic lights made long smeared trails of color on the wet pavements. At last we pulled up in front of a simple Italian restaurant. A neon sign flashed, Pizza—Take-out.

Rob parked, then looked at me, suddenly uncertain. "We could go someplace else if you don't like this place."

"No, I love Italian food." I remembered that Isabel had liked expensive restaurants, and for a second I wondered if I had made a stupid mistake. But then I relaxed. After all, I told myself, pretty much everybody likes Italian food. I should quit worrying about small details. I was doing okay.

Inside, the hostess seated us at a small table. A brisk waitress took our order and hurried away at once. A candle in a glass chimney shed a flickering light on the red plastic tablecloth. Rob reached past the candle and clasped my hands in his. "It's not my imagination, is it, that you seem more centered?"

"No, I guess I am."

The cleft in his chin deepened as he smiled. "Maybe everything's going to be great from now on, huh? And don't tell me nothing is perfect, because I already know that. Only I don't want to think about it tonight."

"Oh, I forgot to bring your ring!" I cried. "I meant to give it back to you tonight."

Rob released my hands. "Don't do that. I want you to keep it."

"No, I'll give it back to you."

"I don't know how I got mixed up with Amy Rose. That stuff about her stealing my ring was weird."

"Amy Rose *is* weird. She leads that coven,

Rob. I looked up eglantine in the dictionary, and it turns out it's a kind of rose, like in her name." I didn't want to tell him how frightened I had been by the package. Now I was embarrassed to remember it. I shot him a quick glance. "I'm not hurting your feelings talking about her this way, am I?"

"I'm not hung up on her, if that's what you're asking."

"I think the coven is meeting in the gazebo at my house."

"You're putting me on!"

I shook my head. "No, really. They've planted herbs around the place and drawn circles in chalk on the floor. I could hear them chanting in the middle of the night. I don't know how many people were out there, but it was quite a few, I think."

"You're sure?"

I nodded.

"You ought to call the cops. If they're meeting on your land, that's trespassing. You could get the cops to watch out for them. It's not like they'd have to be there every night. You can tell them when the meetings are because Amy puts up those notices at school."

"I doubt if trespassing is a big deal for the police."

"Then we could stake it out ourselves. Carl would help us."

"I don't know if that's such a good idea. I don't want any trouble"

Rob shrugged. "It's up to you. But it would give me the creeps to have that bunch meeting in my backyard. Who knows what they're up to?"

"You think they're doing something illegal?"

"If they're not, why are they sneaking around? I don't know how I got mixed up with Amy Rose." Rob shook his head. "I guess I went a little crazy when you and I broke up."

I squeezed his hands. "It doesn't matter."

"When I think about it, Amy Rose is everything I can't stand in a girl," Rob said. "She manipulates people—okay, sometimes they're just begging for it—but on top of it, she flat out lied to me."

The waitress brought steaming plates of spaghetti and laid them before us. I felt too queasy to eat mine. Nothing Amy Rose had done to Rob was as bad as what I had done to him.

"Iz!"

I looked up to see Jane with a blond boy who

towered over her. I remembered that she had mentioned at lunch that a basketball player had asked her out. "Hi." I smiled at them.

"I didn't expect to see you here," Jane said, her eyes accusing me.

Too late, I realized that Isabel would have called Jane and told her about her upcoming dinner date with Rob. It hadn't even occurred to me to do that. I couldn't get used to the idea of having a best friend. And I hadn't been over to visit Jane's mother either. Now she really would think I was cooling on the friendship after all.

"Hey, you guys remember Biff Wilson, don't you?" said Jane. "The coach tells him carbohydrates are the way to go, so Biff is eating double orders of spaghetti."

"I'm lifting weights, too," said Biff. "Three times a week."

Biff began outlining his training program in detail, and I watched Rob's eyes glaze over. I had been wondering if we should ask Jane and Biff to join us, but when I saw Rob's expression, I gave up on the idea.

"I guess we'd better grab ourselves a table," said Jane. Her pocketbook slipped out her grasp, and we all dove for it at once. I felt a thump against my head as my own purse spun out of sight. Rubbing our bumped heads, we all laughed.

A determined waitress bore down on us, claimed Jane and Biff, and led them to another table.

"Jeez, I thought they were going to try to butt in here," Rob said darkly. "Imagine listening to Biff talk about lifting weights all night. I hope Jane doesn't strangle him."

"She's probably got more patience than you do."

Rob retrieved my pocketbook from where it had been kicked under a chair. I saw him glance at the letter that had tumbled out of it before he stuffed it back in my purse. "I see you're writing to your mother," he said, handing it back to me.

"Y-yes," I admitted. It seemed to me that I could field this one easily. Isabel never *had* written Mother, but she could have. Rob sat down across from me and gave me a piercing look. "Iz, have you been in therapy over the summer?"

"W-why do you ask?" I stuttered.

He shrugged. "Well, you sort of hinted you were working through a lot of things. So I figured . . ." He glanced up at me. "It's nothing to be ashamed of, you know. It's not like it's any disgrace."

I couldn't meet his level gaze, and instead I found myself staring down at my plate of spaghetti.

"You should have done it years ago," he said. "All that rage at your mother was hurting you a lot more than it was hurting her, right?"

"Yes, I can see that." I gulped. I had had no inkling until now that Isabel had been angry at Mom. The outpouring of emotion seemed curiously lopsided, since I knew that Mom scarcely ever gave her a thought. But maybe that was what had bothered Isabel, the casualness of the abandonment. I felt stupid for not realizing it. At least in my case I could tell myself that my father was so eccentric that he wasn't much of a loss. It must have been different for Isabel. Maybe she had even worried that she had been left behind with him because there was something wrong with her.

"Don't you feel better now that you've broken the ice with your mom?" Rob asked.

"I guess." I smoothed the napkin in my lap self-consciously.

"And your dad—it seems like things between you two are better, too. Less smothery close, if you know what I mean. Maybe he's starting to realize you've got your own life."

"Maybe."

I was horrified when Rob lifted my hand and brushed his lips against my fingers. "I love you, Iz," he said hoarsely. "I've been trying not to, but I can't help it." His eyes met mine. "What's wrong? Have I scared you or something?"

I nodded mutely.

"Is that because you love me, too?" he asked, his mouth twisting. "Or because you don't?"

"Because I do," I whispered.

He laughed suddenly. "Well, all right, then. That's good, right?"

I imagined breaking the truth to him and felt sick.

"And don't go telling me nothing's perfect, okay?" He shook his head. "Don't you dare rain on my parade."

Why was I going on with this masquerade? It was one thing to pretend to be Isabel when it was only a game; it was another thing entirely to look at Rob straight-faced and lie to him. "Excuse me," I said suddenly. I jumped up and fled to the ladies' room.

Groping my way past some latticework and fake ivy, I found myself in a cool corridor that led directly to the outside parking lot. Here attempts at decor vanished. A bucket on wheels was parked in the hallway next to a mop, and a damp, asphalt-flavored breeze blew through the open door leading to the parking lot. I pressed my hand to my chest and tried to make myself breathe evenly. I could walk out that back door, I reminded myself, and never come back. None of this was for real, which meant I could step out of this game with no penalty as easily as if I were folding a bad hand in a game of poker. Except for Rob. I admitted to myself that Rob was the reason I was in no hurry to walk away.

The door from the restaurant to the corridor swung open and Jane came in. "What's going on with you and Rob?" she whispered. "I could see him grabbing your hands. He's so intense! He looked like he was about to propose."

I stared at her blankly.

"You aren't telling me he *did* propose?" she breathed, horrified.

"No, but I guess I have to admit that we're more than just friends."

"I told you that you couldn't pull that one off." Jane chuckled suddenly.

"I don't even want to be just friends," I said, thinking out loud. "Rob is too important to me."

Jane's eyes had widened. "I thought you said that you would never go head over heels for him."

I felt a rush of relief that Isabel hadn't loved Rob. I wasn't stealing him from her after all.

"Is this smart, Iz?" asked Jane earnestly. "Are you sure you want to get in so deep? You know how you two fight. I just don't want you to be miserable." She hesitated. "You aren't still having trouble with that memory loss you were telling us about, are you?"

I laughed. Here I was thinking that I was falling in love, and Jane was hinting that my problem was brain damage. "I don't know if it's smart or not." I shook my head. "I just can't stop myself."

"You two have always had a weird kind of relationship—very off and on," said Jane, shrugging a little. "I guess you'll just keep on that way, huh?"

"I guess," I said. I wondered if Isabel had told Jane the whole truth about her feelings.

Jane put her hands on my shoulders and looked into my eyes. "Just promise me you won't do anything you can't get out of, okay?"

I grinned. "I won't marry him. I promise you that." For one thing, I could hardly sign a marriage license with Isabel's name.

"You know what I mean," she said severely. "Don't get so serious. Remember that just a few months ago you were screaming that you never wanted to see the guy again."

"I must have been out of my mind," I said.

"I guess it's a case of you can't get along with each other and you can't get along without each other, right?" she suggested.

That wasn't my problem, but I said, "Yeah."

Two little girls skipped past us, wearing short pleated skirts held up with suspenders. They were holding hands, and I saw that their hair was held back from their faces with yellow barrettes in the shape of ducks. I watched them as if they were a foreign language I was trying to decipher. They went into the ladies' room together, giggling. It was my own life I was trying to work out, I realized— mine and, in some tangled way, Isabel's. I felt I had gotten on a merry-go-round and it had speeded up until I was dizzy and sick but afraid to jump off. I had never been so drawn to a boy in my life.

I made my way back to the table. When Rob looked up at me and smiled, I felt as if I had just gone past the last exit on the turnpike. The signposts had disappeared, and I wasn't sure what came next.

"You know what this is like?" Rob said, as I sat down. "It's like when you look out over a race course and all you see are high fences and ditches and dark stretches. Then suddenly—bang! It all falls down and there's a straight stretch of road."

"Like hitting a bunch of green lights you don't expect," I offered.

"Yeah." He grinned.

Too many green lights could be dangerous, I realized suddenly. It was very possible to end up where I had never intended to go.

CHAPTER 10

During the next week, Rob got in the habit of coming by in his old car to pick me up for long drives. We talked with an easy comfortableness, and we touched each other a lot, almost as if we were afraid this new thing between us wouldn't last. That's what I was feeling, anyway. What we had together was important and precious, but I knew the first breath of truth would blow it away.

It was always a relief to leave my father's house and to drive off, trailing black smoke and listening to the clunk of Rob's old car as it changed gears. Usually we ended up at Battlefield Park, leaving the car just past the tall white monument that stood by the parking lot. We were close enough to the river to see a thin rim of bright water through the tangle of bushes. There was a waterfall but it sounded distant, like the rumor of a long-ago battle. The overhanging trees and the roar of the falls made for privacy, and judging from the line of cars that gathered under the trees in the evenings, it was a popular place.

Being close to Rob felt entirely right, as if I had come home after a long journey. I liked to bury my nose in the hollow of his shoulder and inhale his smell. Just being close to him made me happy. But I suppose the oddest thing about the time we spent together was the way all the questions about the summer's burglary, Amy Rose, and whether or not I'd been in therapy simply melted away. When we were together, none of that seemed to matter.

One Sunday afternoon, we found ourselves clambering along the nature walk that ran beside the secluded woods beyond the falls. Parts of the trail were rocky and slick with damp moss. The trail wound in a long loop, eventually returning to where it had begun. When we got back to the parking lot we were hot. I could feel sweat on my upper lip and wet circles marked the underarms of Rob's shirt. The falls drowned out the sound of the passing cars that were visible on the main road just beyond the entrance.

"Iz!" Rob cried suddenly, his grip on me tightening. "Did you see that?"

"What?"

"That car! I swear that looked like your car going by."

It took me a second to pull myself together enough to speak. "Are you sure?"

"How can I be sure? It went by so fast. But how many orange Volvos can be on the road? I've never seen another one, have you? I thought I spotted the Save the Whales bumper sticker, too. Some kind of purple sticker, anyhow."

"You're frightening me," I whispered.

"I guess there isn't much point in calling the police," Rob said as he guided me toward his car. He wiped his damp brow with his hand and frowned. "If the burglars are stupid enough to drive it around here, somebody else is bound to see it sooner or later. We ought to keep an eye out and try to get a look at the license plate. If we're sure it's the right car, then we'll call the cops."

His old car coughed in protest as we backed out of the parking place and pulled onto the main road. "You aren't freaking out about this, are you, Iz?" he asked.

I closed my eyes, trying not to think about

Isabel's bloodied face. Suddenly, though I was hugging myself, my arms felt cold. I unbuckled my seat belt and scooted over closer to Rob.

He grinned. "There's a seat belt in the middle."

I fished the seat belt out of the cushions and buckled it. When we pulled up to a red light, we kissed, and I was afraid to stop. "Iz," Rob said suddenly, "do you ever have the feeling this isn't quite real?"

I stiffened. "What do you mean?"

"I don't know." Rob raked his fingers through my hair carelessly and smiled at me. The light changed and he returned his attention to the road.

"You must have been thinking of something when you said that," I insisted.

"It's just guilt." He grinned. "You know how my mom says that everything fun is either illegal, immoral, or fattening? I guess I feel like if I'm this happy, I must be doing something wrong."

"You're not doing anything wrong," I said, holding him tightly. I was the one who was doing something wrong.

We drove beyond town, passing car lots, building supply stores, and stretches of empty highway. Soon we saw only trees and the high phone wires that lined the road. Then Rob's car turned onto the lane that ended in my father's driveway. I always parked the Corvette in the driveway, never bothering to pull it into the big garage that lay adjacent to my father's study. It was almost as if I expected I'd have to make a quick getaway.

Today my father must not have ventured to the road to get the mail. A colored plastic disk was attached to the mailbox, so that when the mail carrier opened the box the disk fell out and signaled the mail's arrival. The disk was dangling loosely on its string now, swinging in the breeze.

"Stop," I said. "I have to get the mail." I leaped out of the car and flipped the box open. I was startled to see only one sheet of folded paper inside. The handwriting was eerily familiar. Isabel's! "Keep your hands off Rob!" it said.

I was vaguely conscious that wind was ruffling the page in my hands and sweeping my hair into my eyes. The car's motor idled behind me, and I could feel my blood pounding in my ears like a drum. Quickly I folded the paper and stuffed it into the pocket of my jeans.

"Is that all you got?" asked Rob when I climbed back in the car. "One letter? We always get tons of junk mail." He reached over to smooth my hair out of my face. The rough warmth of his palm seemed strange, far removed from the cold panic that had chilled me. "Iz," he said, "don't let that junk with the car get to you, okay? Chances are it wasn't even your car. Probably some respectable salesman from Ohio was driving it. I wish I hadn't told you about it."

"No, I'm glad you did," I said, shivering. "This way I can be watching out." I realized that the sheet of paper must have been put in after the mail carrier had come. No stamp was on it. It had been hand-delivered.

Rob pulled up behind my car in the driveway, then jumped out and trotted around to my side of the car. When I got out, he flung his arms around me, imprisoning me in a tight embrace. He grinned. "I want to kiss you," he said. "Do you suppose your creepy father is watching us?" He flushed. "I mean your nice old father. Sorry about that. I still have to work on a few things."

"He probably is." I glanced at the window. "He must have heard us drive up."

"We aren't going to let that stop us, are we?" He kissed me but must have felt me stiffen, because he abruptly released me and pulled away, his eyes darkening. "I'm really sorry I scared you. I feel like such a jerk. I just didn't think about how traumatized you had been by that attack at the beach."

I glanced over my shoulder and shivered. "I better go in." It seemed years ago, in a dimly remembered lifetime, that Rob and I had been walking on the nature trail, talking happily, making stupid jokes. Now all I wanted was to get inside and lock the doors.

Rob walked me up to the door and gave me a peck that tickled the top of my head. "I'll call you later, okay?"

I nodded and darted inside. It was a relief to get out of Rob's sight, where I didn't have to pretend to be a sane person. I was wild with terror and could feel cold sweat trickling down my back. I ran upstairs to my room, pulled the folded sheet of paper out of my pocket with trembling fingers, and spread it out on the desk. Isabel's handwriting! Who could recognize it better than I, who had spent so much time practicing it? "Keep your hands off Rob!"

My skin seemed to shrink. I had the awful sensation that Isabel's spirit had been standing outside the car at Battlefield Park watching Rob and me as we made out. *Isabel is dead,* I told myself. But I wondered why I hadn't noticed before how vividly she was present in this room, so different from the other rooms of my father's house. This room shrieked color and luxury. Everything from the pretty flowered rug to the closet stuffed with clothes and the exuberant poster on the wall spoke of a personality too vivid to die. The chess set, the elaborately inlaid game table, the stuffed animals jammed cheek to jowl on the top shelf of the closet—chipmunks, Mr. Jeremy Fisher, an owl, a mouse in a red jacket. The room was rich with Isabel's personality.

Yet Isabel *was* dead. My nerveless fingers smoothed out the note before me on the desk. Then how could I be holding Isabel's message in my hands? Impossible. Ghosts didn't exist.

Suddenly a possible explanation hit me, and I felt weak with relief. Suppose Isabel had written this very note to Amy Rose! And then suppose Amy Rose had saved it and put it in my mailbox. That made sense.

Or did it? Amy Rose had no way of knowing how unnerving it would be for me to get a note from Isabel because Amy Rose didn't know that Isabel was dead. I gripped the edge of the desk suddenly, afraid I would slip to the ground in a dead faint. *Unless Amy Rose had killed her.* The words sounded in my brain like an alarm.

I must have sat frozen for several seconds before I realized that the desk's decorated rim had moved in my grip. I glanced down along the fragile border, where matchstick-sized pieces of dark wood were inlaid in the veneer in the shape of chess pieces and suits of cards. My first impression was that in my agitation I had grabbed the edge too hard and broken it. Maybe the decorative rim had become unglued. I hooked my fingers around the bottom of it and pulled gently to test it. To my astonishment the wood opened out. The intricate veneer turned out to be the outside of a hidden drawer that slid out easily. Lying against the pale wood of its interior was a notebook-sized black computer. I had no difficulty recognizing it as Isabel's Wiz.

The computer sat on top of its instruction book. I lifted it, turned at once to the page headed "alarm function," and followed the instructions for turning off the alarm. At least my sleep would not be disturbed by the buzzer tonight—assuming that I could ever sleep again.

I caught a glimpse of my image in the mirror through the open bathroom door and saw that my face was white and my eyes were round with fear. One thing was certain. I could not tell Rob about the note I had found in the mailbox. I couldn't tell him that Amy Rose had committed murder without telling him that I wasn't Isabel. If Amy Rose was threatening me, I had to handle it on my own. Only I wasn't quite sure how.

I turned the small computer over, certain now that the Wiz must have been what the burglar—Amy Rose, perhaps?—had been looking for when the house got ransacked. It all made sense if the Wiz held the secret to Isabel's murder.

I was not the big fan of computers that Isabel had been, and it took me some time to figure out, with the help of the instruction booklet, how to work the thing. But at last I managed to make it give up its files. To my disappointment, nothing interesting appeared on the small screen—just lists of telephone numbers, things to do, a calendar. Mocking me all the while was the small "s" in the corner of the display screen that told me the little computer held secret files that could not be read without a password.

I heard the musical ding of the doorbell. I waited for my father to answer it, but it only rang again more insistently.

I went out into the hall and looked out the window. A UPS truck was idling in the driveway. Directly below me, at the front door, a young man in uniform leaned on the doorbell. By no stretch of the imagination did he look like Amy Rose in disguise. I ran downstairs and opened the door. "You have to sign for this," he said, extending a clipboard. I signed Isabel's name. "Thanks," he said. He ran down the steps and back to his truck while I stared at the large box at my feet. It was addressed to my father and had the return address, "Farmingdale Funeral Home."

I got the large package inside the house, then took a knife from the kitchen and slit the packing tape. Inside was a squat pottery urn with a top that had been carefully sealed with what looked like wax. A white temporary label fixed to the urn said "Remains of Isabel Herrick." Isabel's ashes! It had never occurred to me to wonder what had happened to her after the cremation. I knew I could never leave this package at the front door for my father to find. The shock might kill him.

I got the urn out of the box and carried it upstairs. I was able to squeeze it onto the bottom shelf of the linen closet. I stuffed the sheets and towels it displaced under my bed. Then I ran downstairs to the kitchen, cut the cardboard box into strips, and stuffed them into a plastic bag. I forced myself to take the bag outside to the garbage, but my back tingled the whole time, as if I could feel the gaze of the unseen Amy Rose. I dashed back in the house, my breath coming in quick pants.

Amy Rose killed Isabel, I thought, *and all that's left of her now are the ashes and bone shards in the urn upstairs.* I hiccuped and wondered if I would burst into uncontrollable crying.

The door to my father's study opened. His tall figure was silhouetted against the bright light of the windows behind him. "Who was that at the door just now?" he asked.

I blinked at him. "The UPS carrier. He had the wrong house." I ran upstairs before he could ask any more questions.

It occurred to me that my father might be able to guess what password Isabel had used. Then I realized that if Isabel had been keeping her diary in a secret file, one of the people she would wish to keep it a secret from was our father. The computer blinked "Password?" I only wished I knew it! The instructions told me the machine would take passwords of six letters or less. A staggering number of words in the English language had six letters or less. And there was no guarantee that the password was even in English.

I tried the obvious one, exactly six letters, and typed ISABEL. "Wrong password," the computer scolded me. I tried again with the word SECRET, again six letters. Wrong Password. I had no better luck with the name of Isabel's favorite color— red—or our birthday or the words chess, Vette, and Wiz. I tried all the pieces on the chessboard and all the suits of cards with no luck.

The phone rang. I picked it up as if in a trance and heard Rob's voice. "Iz?" he said. "How do you feel?"

"Like a nervous wreck." My voice trembled.

"You want me to come over and stay with you awhile?"

And have my father rubbing his hands gleefully when Rob showed up? No thanks. I cleared my throat. "No, I'll be okay, Rob. I've just got to pull myself together." *If you were Isabel and trying to think up a password, what would you use?* I thought. But I didn't say that out loud, of course. It was almost scary how I had gotten used to not saying what I was thinking.

"I don't guess you've heard from your mother," Rob said.

"No. The letter has barely had time to get there."

"What about your sister?"

"My sister?" My mouth went suddenly dry.

"I thought you two had been writing. Aren't you still hearing from Liz?"

"Yes," I choked. "We're sort of getting to know each other."

"That must be weird, having a twin you've never met. What do you think she's like? I mean, as a person."

I hesitated. "Sensible."

He laughed. "You make her sound boring."

"She doesn't have roots in a particular place, like me." I took a deep breath. "So she's had to find a balance inside herself."

"I guess you'd describe me as sensible, too," Rob said, not sounding too happy about it.

I smiled. "No, I'd describe you as wonderful."

He laughed and seemed pleased. "I don't see why she doesn't just fly over here and visit you. What's the big deal?"

"It's not that easy. She's got her own life. Our mother's not keen on the idea of us getting to know each other, and she's kind of afraid of our father."

"She told you all that?"

"I can read between the lines," I said. I wished we would talk about some less dangerous subject, but I was afraid of being too obvious about wrenching the conversation away from my sister.

"Anyway, you can get together when she comes over for college. You are still planning to go to college together, aren't you?"

"Yes," I croaked.

"Iz, you sound terrible. Are you sure you're okay? Maybe I ought to come over."

"No! No, don't do that. I've got all kinds of homework, Rob. I'll be fine. I'm just kind of on edge."

"It's all my fault," he said dolefully.

"No, no," I protested. "I'll be all right." It hadn't hit me until that moment that Isabel must have been thinking about me as much as I had been thinking about her. I stared fixedly at the computer, where her secrets were hidden. Seized suddenly by a hunch, I propped the receiver under my chin. Balancing the Wiz on my lap I awkwardly typed the password LIZ.

The little machine made tiny clunking noises. Suddenly thirty lines of print appeared on the display screen. "I'd better go now, Rob," I said breathlessly. "I've really got to get down to that homework."

"Okay," said Rob. He sounded uneasy. "Bye."

"Bye," I said. After I hung up, I gazed at the tiny computer screen with deep satisfaction.

December 26—I have decided to try keeping my diary on the Wiz.

I had found Isabel's secret password!

CHAPTER 11

My own name was the password to Isabel's secret diary! I felt as if that meant she were giving me permission to read it. I hooked the Wiz up to the printer with a cable and typed in the print command. After a moment's hesitation, the printer made quick zipping sounds and began spitting out pages. As fast as the paper rolled into my hands, I read Isabel's words.

I got another sweet but bland letter from Liz today. It's odd to think how outclassed I felt when we first started writing. Just because she's been to Nepal and knows people who live in castles and can speak French, I thought she would be one up on me. But it's so obvious to me now that what makes people stars isn't what they've *done,* but who they *are.* Liz and I might look alike, but it's like comparing plain glass to the shimmering crystal prisms of a chandelier. Liz doesn't have the complexity to be an interesting person. One life is enough for her; I need at least three!

It'll be cool when we get together at college, though. Maybe I could get her to pretend to be me when we come home together. She could even go out with Rob. I wonder if he could tell the difference? Switching places is a delicious idea, but something tells me I'll have to lead up to it gradually. All signs point to Liz being very straight. What she needs is for her sister to show her how to have a good time!

My cheeks burned as I read Isabel's words. She never could have guessed that I would read those lines or foreseen that I would end up doing just what she had planned. We *had* switched places, but it hadn't been a cheerful prank. I thought of her cold ashes in the linen closet only yards away from where I was standing and felt a tremor of nausea.

It was hard not to be put off by her thinking that she was better than me, but I quickly reminded myself that we were raised differently. All my life I'd had to tag along after my sociable and amusing mother, while Isabel had the undivided attention of her adoring father. Naturally I had ended up with a more humble opinion of my place in the world than Isabel had. Besides, what she said was true. In Sewell's Falls Isabel *was* a star.

The next entry was dated several days later. I noticed that she didn't write every day. It was as if she waited until she could feel exclamation points of excitement bursting out of her before she picked up the Wiz and began to type:

I am having the most utterly cool time! When I'm with Blackie, the edge of danger sets my heart racing. Last night he was waiting for me at the gazebo, his breath making clouds in the still night air. This is the first time I've let him know where I live, and he looked at the house with a stare that was spooky. If I come home some night and find all the computers missing, then I'll know he was casing it. The moon was hiding behind a halo of mist, and the frosty ground crackled under our shoes as we walked to the bike. He parked some distance away on the road because he's always worried about the bike falling on its side. Falling does something awful to it, apparently. It was a cold night for meeting him at the gazebo, but its not as if he could come to the front door. If Dad knew about Blackie, he would kill me. We went to an all-night place called the Chicken Shack that's been condemned by the Board of Health. I ate french fries and absolutely nothing else. I don't care if Blackie murders me and mutilates my body, but I refuse to die of salmonella poisoning. It would be *too* humiliating. After we ate he rolled up his sleeve and showed me his new tattoo. It was all pink and puffy around blue dots in the shape of a cobra. Disgusting, but at the same time a strange sort of turn-on. "So appropriate," I purred. He frowned and said, "What do you mean by that?" I wasn't sure whether the word *appropriate* was too big for him or whether he's getting defensive now that he knows I live in a big house. "It's a compliment," I said. "I like dangerous guys." Sometimes it's hard to figure out whether Blackie is the strong silent type, or whether he's just lacking in the brains department. I burned my leg on the bike's exhaust pipe riding back to the house and had to wear tights to school today to hide the burn. It gives me a kick to realize that nobody at school even knows that guys like Blackie exist. I feel like an Old Soul, sucking up knowledge of good and evil.

The printer continued to zip along as I stared at the page. Isabel's tone puzzled me—a mixture of flippancy and intensity. I could tell she had enjoyed the drama of meeting Blackie on the sly. What I couldn't figure out was whether she had some real reason to be afraid of him.

There was a big gap in the diary and then several pages devoted to a bizarre murder that had hit the newspapers in late February. A husband had murdered his wife and put her body in a freezer in a rental storage bin. The crime had only come to light two years later, when the murderer's second wife failed to pay the mini-storage company's monthly rental fee. The compartment had been opened, and its owner had called the police.

Isabel seemed fascinated by the murderer's carelessness. "You'd think this was one bill he'd pay himself" was her comment. The case struck a chord, evidently, and led her to recount similar crimes going back over the past twenty years. If I could believe Isabel, men who stashed their wives' bodies in freezers were commonplace. One thing was certain—the true-crime magazines I had found in the corner of her room had been carefully read. Isabel was a scholar of crime. Lurid, sensational crime.

There were no entries for weeks after that, but in March Isabel's attention had been caught by a sensational murder case involving cults and torture. I skipped distastefully over her sickeningly detailed account. The police had issued a statement saying that the murderer, though involved in cult activities, had been motivated by a love triangle. I found myself thinking of Amy Rose. I couldn't understand why Isabel would want to read about this stuff. I felt that I was seeing her dark side—a strange, obsessive interest in evil.

I spotted Jane's name and skipped ahead to it.

Jane said the other day that I'm always "on." It's true that I work hard at being friendly so nobody can say I'm stuck up. But there was an edge to what she said, and I didn't know quite how to take it. I think she's jealous, which is ironic. I used to be jealous of her because she had such a great mother. All those cupcakes and peanut butter sandwiches and handmade dresses for our chubby plastic dolls. And now Mrs. C. can't even comb her own hair. Yesterday when I was over there, I had to give her a glass of water. When she drank she slobbered on herself. I just kept talking about school and wiped off her face as if what had happened was the most ordinary thing in the world, but I could see tears in her eyes. I felt like crying, too. It's so sad.

I realized that Isabel had been genuinely fond of Jane's mother. The odd thing was how seldom any sort of tenderness showed up in the diary. I skimmed ahead. Rob's name popped up enough that it was clear he was a fixture in her life. But if she'd ever clearly outlined her feelings about him, she had done it before Christmas when this diary began. I found myself thinking that she took him for granted, but I knew that wasn't fair to her. This part of her diary covered only a comparatively brief space of time. What I was reading was only a thin slice of Isabel's life, not the whole story.

Rob was certainly not the only boy mentioned. It would have been interesting from a personal, as well as a scientific standpoint, to know exactly what sort of shimmering signals she had sent out that had been so attractive. "I think he likes me," was a monotonous refrain in the diary. In another place she wrote, "I know how to make people feel good." Maybe her knack for attracting boys was only that. But I had the feeling that there was a different side to it. Isabel *needed* admiration. It was as if it filled an empty space inside her.

Reading on, I learned that she was curious about other people's secrets. Whenever I'd stumbled onto secrets, I'd been embarrassed, but it was clear that Isabel had felt differently. Maybe, for her, secrets had been the proof that she and another person had made a special connection. I thought of the cold home life she must have had with our father and decided she might have needed that feeling of closeness.

Tom Detweiler told me in art class today that he's never learned to read. I think that's the worst secret anybody's ever told me. He has to take care of his little sister in the afternoons because his mother works. Just hearing about his life gave me chills, as if I was the one trapped in it. He missed three days of school because his father died last week. He was really upset, and I guess that's why all this came tumbling out while we were working on our charcoal sketches. I think people talk to me because I'm interested. I suppose I know more secrets than anybody in the school.

It's amazing how much I find out by picking up things that get thrown away. Some kids don't even bother to put a lock on their lockers. Jennifer left a whole stack of her boyfriend's letters in her locker. After I read a few, I could see why she didn't want to take them home. And I found a bottle of diet pills in Phyl Dinty's locker. She knows you're supposed to go to the office if you want to take so much as an aspirin. How could she be so careless?

When I read the label on the bottle, I felt a weird surge of power, thinking of how I could get Phyl into a lot of trouble if I wanted, but I put the pills back in her locker real fast. As it happens, I like Phyl, but I think it was pretty stupid of her to give somebody that kind of hold on her.

It's not just kids either. I was in the teacher's lounge yesterday, delivering a message, and I found an overdraft notice and a charge card bill in the wastebasket. Mrs. Draper is overdrawn at the bank by a hundred dollars, and Mrs. Henson had a charge slip from someplace called "Peek-a-boo Undies." I hate to imagine Mrs. Henson in frilly underwear. She's forty if she's a day and could stand to lose a few pounds. Utterly revolting. I could probably make a fortune if I were interested in blackmail, but I'm not. I just like to *know*. I suppose it makes me feel one up on people to know more about them than they know about me.

I blinked at the image of Isabel rifling through lockers and wastebaskets. Didn't it occur to her that if she got caught snooping, someone would have found out *her* dirty little secret?

But the very next passage reminded me that Isabel might have stumbled onto something with all her poking around.

Amy Rose was reading a book during algebra today. Just trying to be friendly, I said, "Must be an interesting book." She showed her teeth—in a nicer person it would have been a smile—and said, "*The Magic Arts*. It's kind of a handbook." I think she must have had a comic book hidden inside it, because the book looked a hundred years old and deadly dull. Amy Rose will do anything to get attention. I've watched the way she gets other kids to hang around with her, and it's like she hypnotizes them. There's no other explanation—she is so bizarre, I don't see how anybody could possibly like her for herself. I've seen her looking at Rob, which is a laugh. Rob would never go for anybody as strange as Amy Rose. I don't exactly like it that she's got her eye on him, though. Sometimes I wonder how far that girl would go to get what she wants.

The printer stopped abruptly and I glanced up startled, then realized it was finished. But I hadn't gotten past the month of April or found out exactly what it was that Isabel had discovered about Amy Rose. With a sinking heart, I realized that there must be other files and other passwords.

I stared at the blank screen, frustrated by the small "s" at the corner of the screen that told me it still held secrets. Exiting the file, I racked my brain for some other password to try. I typed OSCAR. Wrong password. ROB. Wrong password.

Suddenly to my amazement letters I had not typed began appearing one by one on the computer's blank screen, as if an unseen hand were pressing the keys. FIND MY KILLER!

I stared at the screen. I laid the computer down on the desk and backed away from it, looking around the room as if I had never seen it before. The continuous roll of paper from the printer lay curled on the rug. The lamp beside the chessboard cast shadows on the desk. Isabel's favorite sweater was draped over the chair. Something hard rattled against the windowpane and I jumped, my teeth chattering. It was as if my twin's personality had been dismembered and strewn over her room, and the cold wind teasing the back of my neck threatened to gather her pieces and return Isabel to life.

I dashed out into the hallway in a panic. The wind sighed in the eaves of the attic. I heard laughter, and the back of my neck prickled. The silvery, high laugh sounded again, then died away into the sound of the wind. Suddenly the doorbell rang.

I ran to the front window and pressed my fingers against it. Condensation dripped down the pane below my fingertips, and my hot breath misted on the glass. I rubbed a clear spot and saw Rob's car parked in the driveway. He had been worried enough about me to come over.

I stumbled down the stairs, threw open the front door, and fell into his arms, sobbing.

"Hey, hey, hey," he said softly. "It's okay. I'm here."

I wiped the tears from my eyes and struggled to catch my breath. "I think I hurt my ankle coming down the stairs." Now that I was calmer, I was a little embarrassed about crying.

Rob scooped me up in his arms. I rested my head on his chest and let the tears stream down my cheeks. "I'm sorry," I babbled. "I feel so stupid."

He opened the car door with one hand and gently slid me into the passenger seat. I wiped my nose and sniffled. "I don't know what's the matter with me." Skidding leaves made a scraping sound on the pavement, and the high wind whistled in the treetops. With the door open, bits of paper whirled around inside the car like confetti.

Rob sank to one knee beside me, looking troubled. "Iz, are you having flashbacks or something? I mean about the stuff that happened this summer?"

I shook my head. "Let's get something to eat. I'll be all right."

"Okay." He squeezed my hand, stood up, and slammed the car door shut.

The wind was an omen, I thought, a sign of spirits. I heard it whistling past the open car door as Rob got in. He switched on the lights, and they shone on the back of the Corvette, kindling its taillights.

My hands rested on the worn knees of my jeans. I reminded myself that everyone who knew me considered me a sensible person. I could *not* be imagining things.

As we backed out, I shot Rob an anxious glance. "Do you believe in ghosts?"

"Nope. What's going on, Iz? I thought you were scared about the burglars. What's all this about ghosts?"

Suddenly I knew I had to tell him what had just happened. I was too freaked out to keep it to myself. I took a deep breath. "You know that little computer that I have?"

He nodded. "The Wiz."

"Tonight something came on the screen that I hadn't typed. It said, 'Find my killer.'" I swallowed hard.

"Are you sure?" he asked.

"What do you mean 'am I sure?' I *saw* it."

"Sometimes when people are upset, they see things that aren't really there," Rob said carefully.

"You think I'm crazy, but I'm not." Did people know if they were going crazy, I wondered with sudden misgiving. Maybe all those people who insisted they were Napoleon and could plug themselves into electric sockets felt they were sensible, too. "If I were going to imagine something," I went on evenly, "do you think it would be words on a computer screen?"

Rob's eyes crinkled in a smile "Okay, I follow you. You're right. If somebody's going to hallucinate, I'd expect it to be something a little more dramatic. If you're getting weird messages on your computer, then I guess somebody must be playing a trick on you. Jerry Wiggins programmed my calculator to say hello every time I turn it on. Maybe somebody put a message on your computer that was timed to show up later."

But that computer had been hidden in the secret drawer of the desk ever since I had arrived. I was certain of that, because it had woken me every night with its alarm. Nobody could have programmed it.

"Wait a minute!" Rob snapped his fingers. "Can't you send messages on those things? My little sister asked for one for her birthday so she and her friends could write notes to each other in class." He smiled. "Mom and Dad didn't think it was such a great idea."

"Infrared beams," I said slowly. I remembered that my father had said Isabel's little computer could pick up messages from similar units.

"It's a weird sort of message, though, isn't it?" Rob shrugged. "It's not like we know anybody who's been murdered."

But we did—someone close to both of us. Only I couldn't tell him about it. I clutched my knees so tightly that my knuckles were white.

"I guess there are guys out there with a perverted sense of humor," said Rob. "How's that ankle of yours feeling?"

I flexed my foot carefully. "Okay, I guess."

I wondered how far infrared beams from a computer would reach. Not far, probably. Wouldn't the person who sent the message almost have to be nearby? Inside the house, even. I remembered the laughter I had heard and shuddered.

Rob drove to a fast food place. The car next to us was blasting loud music when we got out, yet I could still hear the wind. The traffic light at the corner was swaying in a wide arc. Wind sucked at the glass door, holding it open, so Rob had to force it closed behind us. We got milkshakes and french fries at the counter and sat down.

"Maybe a hurricane is brewing," I said.

"Nah. I heard the weather report driving over. Just thunderstorms and a tornado watch."

Our hands crept closer across the Formica, then touched. "Rob, who would send me a creepy message like that?"

He frowned. "Probably some computer freak. You know those fantasy games they play on computers, the ones with dragons, monsters, and avengers? It sounds like it could be part of that.

Maybe one of those guys has a crush on you. Some people will do anything to get attention."

I started. "Amy Rose will do anything to get attention," Isabel had written. But it didn't make sense for Amy Rose to write that message. If she had killed Isabel, the last thing she would want me to do was to find Isabel's killer.

It must have seemed an eerily familiar sort of evening to Rob, who had once complained that Isabel only seemed half there. My lips formed the proper words, and I cocked my head attentively when he talked about his efforts to get a tutor for calculus and when he told a funny story about something that happened to his mother at work. But all I could think about was the strange message that had appeared on the small computer screen.

Our french fries grew stiff and cold in their thin paper bags. Rob must have realized that I shrank from returning to the house. It was after midnight when he finally took me home.

"You've got a phone by your bed, don't you?" he said when we drove to the house.

I nodded.

"If anything happens, call me. Or the cops."

I nodded. But how could I tell anyone that all I heard was laughter?

CHAPTER 12

I realized I had left the house without my key. The front door opened at once when I turned the knob.

Rob frowned when he saw the door had been left unlocked. "Maybe I'd better go upstairs with you and check things out, just in case."

"You don't have to do that," I said. "My father's been home all night. It's all right." My father was so self-absorbed I wasn't sure he would have noticed if thieves had marched out the front door carrying half the contents of the house, but I didn't tell Rob. I didn't want him to go checking around the house. That meant he'd go into my room and see the curl of paper coming out of the printer and Isabel's words spilling out onto the floor.

A sudden gust of wind caught the front door

and slammed it open. "Don't argue," said Rob, stepping inside. "I'll just have a look around. It'll only take a minute." He ran up the stairs, taking them two at a time.

I pulled the door closed and followed him reluctantly. When I reached my room, I blinked in surprise. The roll of paper had vanished. Disbelieving, I glanced at the desk. The cable that had been connected to the Wiz lay there, but the shiny connecting ring at the end wasn't attached to anything. The Wiz was gone!

I was standing there frozen when Rob strode into the bathroom. "Don't come in here," he said in a strange voice.

I squeezed past him and saw at once what he was staring at. Someone had taken a lipstick and printed on the mirror, "Leave Rob alone."

Rob threw the shower curtain back with a rattle and seemed relieved to find no body in the bathtub.

I backed out of the bathroom and sat heavily on the bed. In my panic to get out of the house, I had never given a thought to locking up. How stupid I had been!

Rob glanced around the room. "I'm going to have to talk to Amy Rose," he said heavily. "I'd better check the rest of the upstairs."

I heard him opening and closing doors out in the hallway, but somehow I was certain he would find no trace of the prowler. Only the small computer had vanished, but for me the room seemed to echo and whistle with emptiness. *Gone. Gone.* The word sounded hopelessly in my brain. The small computer had vanished with all its secrets. If it had contained the motive for Isabel's murder, that was gone, too.

Rob reappeared. "What happened to the mattress in the room across the hall?" he demanded.

"Remember I told you we had a break-in."

"They slashed the mattress in the spare room?" He stared at me. "Why?"

"Actually, that mattress was in my room at the time," I admitted.

"I don't like this, Iz. It's scary." He glanced around and saw the unattached cable. "Where's your little computer? The one that had the message on it?"

"I don't know." I turned my palms up helplessly. "It's gone."

"You stay here, okay? I'm going to check downstairs."

"Don't bother my father!" I warned.

He uttered a fierce epithet as he charged down

the stairs. After a moment, I trailed after him. I could hear him opening doors and closets. His heavy footsteps thundered around the house.

My father appeared at the door of his study in a green satin bathrobe. "What's going on?" he demanded. Bright patches of red stood out on his cheekbones, looking as if veins had broken under the force of strong emotion. "What's this about?"

"Have you seen the Wiz?" I asked. "I left it in my room and now it's gone."

His eyes glittered. "Certainly not. Wasn't the house tightly locked up when you went out?"

"I guess not," I admitted.

"Some opportunistic thief must have come in while you were gone and made off with it. Let this be a lesson to you not to go off gallivanting and leaving the door unlocked."

"But you were here. You must have heard whoever came in."

"Nonsense. With both the doors to my study and my bedroom shut, an intruder would have to make a terrible racket for me to hear him."

I didn't bother to make a sharp retort. Meeting his eyes, I felt myself grow warm with anger. I could see that he was enjoying my distress.

Rob bounded back to my side, panting. "No

sign of anybody anywhere in the house."

My father gave him a look of cold dislike.

Without saying another word, I took Rob's arm and we walked out of the house. Outside, the wind whipped my hair into my eyes and pelted my face until my skin felt numb. The wind changed its pitch as it shifted, making a sad song in the high limbs of the trees.

"You ought to call the cops," Rob said.

I squinted my eyes against blowing grit. "They'll love it that I left the door unlocked, won't they?"

"I don't care what they think. This thing is no joke, Iz. The way that mattress was slashed is sick."

"The mattress got cut in the first burglary," I said. "The police have already seen it, and we've had all the locks changed since then."

Rob ran his fingers through his windblown hair. "What can be going on? It never occurred to me that Amy Rose was actually out of her mind." He rested both his hands on my shoulders. "Iz, tell me the truth. You're not still seeing that guy on the motorcycle, are you?"

I twisted out of his grasp. "You know better than that. I'm with you practically all the time."

"I know," he said unhappily. "Maybe I shouldn't have brought it up. But I just can't picture Amy Rose doing this."

"And I can't believe a boy wrote on that mirror," I said coldly. "A boy wouldn't think to write a message with lipstick."

"What was the motorcycle guy's name?"

"Blackie."

"Blackie what?"

I shrugged. "I don't know. Just Blackie."

"Whatever happened to him?"

"I don't know." I thrust my cold fingers into the pockets of my jeans.

"You're mad at me for mentioning him, aren't you?"

I realized that my shoulders were hunched up, as if I expected a blow from behind, and I glanced uneasily over my shoulder. Grit blew in my eyes and made tears stream down my cheeks. I could see a shadow moving against the closed curtain of my father's study.

"I'm so generally freaked out," I said steadily, "that if I'm mad at you, it's only a little blip in the general mess of things." The wind had dried my tears and left salty streaks that made my cheeks itch. I was unreasonably annoyed at Isabel for going out with Blackie. Our fates were so mingled now, it was hard for me to untwist them. "I'm really scared," I said, meeting Rob's gaze, "And I think you ought to keep that in mind and be nicer to me."

He enfolded me in his arms. "Okay," he said gruffly. "Let's make up, huh? Forget what I said. Are you mad?"

I let my forehead rest on his chest and sniffled loudly as I shook my head. "I can't stay mad at you, Rob. You're too important to me."

He tightened his grip. "Look, tomorrow I'm going to talk to Amy Rose. If you see them dragging me into the office in handcuffs, you'll know I lost my cool and gave her a black eye."

We kissed, but it didn't help. My fingers felt stiff and cold, and I had to remind myself to blink. "I guess I'd better go upstairs and get some sleep," I said at last.

"Yeah," he said. "Lock the house up tight, okay?"

He had already said that once. I knew then that he was as infected with fear as I was. The wind whipped my hair into my eyes as I watched Rob get in his car. I raised my hand and waved goodbye.

When he had gone I went back in the house and made sure that every door and window had been locked. The wind sucked against the glass, making it bend and rattle. I could not bring myself to go into my father's room or his study. I decided to assume that he had secured his part of the house, and I went upstairs.

Opening the bathroom door, I stared at the mirror. The lipsticked message half obscured the image, but I could tell that my eyes were bloodshot. There was no use getting in bed despite the lateness of the hour. I wasn't a bit sleepy.

I got sponges and a plastic bucket from downstairs, then perched on the edge of the bathroom vanity and washed the lipstick off. That way at least I would not have to look at it in the morning. I picked up the broken lipstick with a tissue and carefully deposited it in an envelope, which I tucked into my underwear drawer in case the lipstick had fingerprints on it.

Never had I understood how easily fear turned into anger as when I closed the drawer and stood stiffly staring out my window a moment later. A light had appeared at the gazebo. It was moving but not in quite the way it had been before. This time its movement was more erratic. I decided wind must be swaying the lantern.

I switched off the lamp beside me. With the light off, I knew I couldn't be seen. It was just 2:00 A.M., I realized, glancing at my watch. Furious, I slipped into a dark jacket and rummaged around in Isabel's drawer until I found a cap to pull over my head. Blond hair was too visible. It would have been good if I could have darkened my face as well.

Making my way downstairs, I quietly slipped out of the house, being careful to lock the door behind me and tuck the key securely in my jeans pocket. Leaves went cartwheeling down the driveway. I figured the wind would cover any sound I made as I walked through the woods.

Flags of light shone out of the windows of the house, so I could see well enough to move around without a flashlight. At ground level, I couldn't see the gazebo as clearly as I could from the higher perch of my bedroom window, but I could hear an indistinct murmur of voices. I drew close to the gazebo, then stooped down a little, taking care to keep hidden behind a bush. Peering through the leaves of the bush, I could see that a lantern was hung from a hook on one of the pillars. Amy Rose stood beside it, her face bleached into a white mask by the powerful light. She bent her head slightly so that her hair fell forward over her face, casting it in shadow. I saw that she was reading from a large book. A tape recorder at her feet gave out the sound of a steady drum beat. "Oh, spirits of the West Wind come to us," she called. "Spirits of the North Wind come to us."

Tonight it was easy to believe the wind was infernal. It whistled wildly overhead as if threatening to tear the trees up by the roots.

Something rattled loudly and fell to the ground with a crash, making me jump. The circle of girls stopped dancing and uttered little cries of distress. Amy Rose looked up and seemed to stare directly at me. But if she saw me, she gave no sign. "It's just a shingle falling off the roof," she shouted. "Don't worry."

"I've got something in my contact lens," called a tall thin girl, detaching herself from the circle.

Amy Rose turned off the tape recorder. "Maybe we'd better quit for tonight," she said, raising her voice to be heard. "The spirits obviously heard us. We've raised plenty of wind."

The circle of girls broke up into untidy clumps, talking and giggling. I heard twigs crack as kids climbed down from the gazebo. A voice sounded very close to me. "My dad would kill me if he found out I was out at this time of night."

I was startled by their sudden nearness and took a quick step back. A dry branch snapped under my foot.

"Who's that?" cried another voice.

"It's a spy! Someone's spying on us. Over there!" yelled Amy Rose. "Get her!"

Gasping, I turned and ran blindly through the woods, stumbling and crashing. Branches tore at my face as I dove forward. I had a sharp pain in my side, and my ankle ached as I blundered on. It seemed an eternity before I found myself on the lawn, breathing hard, my clenched fist pressed to my chest. No one charged out of the woods after me, and I could hear the sound of engines starting up in the distance. Standing alone on the lawn, my panic subsiding, I felt suddenly foolish. If they had come after me at all, I realized, they must have given up almost at once. Now I half wished I had stood my ground. They were the ones who were trespassing, not me. But when my heart had begun hammering in fear in the dark woods, it hadn't been much comfort to know that the law was on my side.

Twigs and leaves were caught in my hair, my face was scratched, and my ankle was throbbing. I didn't want my father to see me looking this disheveled. I let myself into the house as quietly as I could, hoping he had gone to bed, then crept silently back upstairs to my room. If Amy Rose had murdered my sister, I reflected bitterly, she was getting away with it.

CHAPTER

When I woke, I could tell it had rained in the night. The trees outside my window were glistening as I threw the windows open. The air felt fresh, rinsed clean, and it had turned cooler. Once at school, I didn't go to homeroom when the bell rang. Instead I went directly to the office and asked to see Mr. Crumpler. I suppose my efforts to cover the scratch on my cheek with makeup hadn't been too effective, because the secretary took one look at me and hurried me back to his office.

"Isabel!" He stared. "What's wrong?"

"Amy Rose is running her coven right out of my backyard," I said. "Can't you notify her parents or something?"

Mr. Crumpler's fingertips met in a steeple

under his chin. I noticed something fleeting in his expression that reminded me of Jane. "What does your father think you should do?" he asked.

"I can't tell him," I said. "He's recovering from a heart attack, and it isn't good for him to get excited."

Mr. Crumpler shook his head. "I wish I could help, Iz, but we don't have any rules against covens in the student handbook. What's more, whatever Amy Rose is up to, she's doing it on her own time and not here. I may not like Amy Rose's influence on other students, but as far as I know she's not doing anything criminal."

"Trespassing is illegal," I countered. "They're meeting on our land. And I think she stole my computer, too."

"Really? Do you have any proof of that?"

I had to admit that I didn't.

He shrugged. "I suppose you could alert the police. Maybe they would keep an eye out for you."

I snorted. The police had not found Isabel's murderer. What were the chances they were anxious to round up Amy Rose for trespassing?

Frowning, I reached for the doorknob. "I thought you'd be glad to have information about what she's doing."

"Naturally we're interested in anything that might be a problem for our students. In fact, I was at a regional meeting last spring where the question of satanic cults came up. But until something happens that's actually illegal, we're helpless."

"You mean Amy Rose can cast spells and do incantations right outside my window, and there isn't a thing I can do about it?"

He shrugged. "Sorry I can't help. Where do you go from here?"

"To my locker," I snapped. Hoisting my backpack over one shoulder, I plodded past the curious secretaries in the front office without a word. When I stepped outside I blinked, bewildered by the light. The campus looked strangely deserted, and I realized it was because everyone else was in homeroom. I stared at a white moth as it fluttered aimlessly past a leaf pasted to the sidewalk. What *was* I going to do now? I didn't know. So far it was almost uncanny the way Amy Rose had outmaneuvered me.

Making my way around the administration building to my locker, I stepped into the swollen shadows cast by the building. I was conscious of someone behind me, but before I had time to turn around, a blinding pain split my head. The sudden wild clangor of the school bell seemed to come from far away, and I was only vaguely aware of falling.

The next thing I noticed were shoes. Hightops. Untied laces. Dirty black tennis shoes. My head hurt so much that I was afraid to move it, and it only slowly dawned on me that I was lying on the sidewalk. I could hear excited voices around me. Painfully, I propped myself up on my elbows. At once I felt sick to my stomach.

"She's coming to," someone cried.

Another voice screeched, "Her face!"

Alarmed, I raised my hands to my face and touched something sticky.

"It's a hex sign," said another voice.

"What?" Confusedly, I struggled to sit up. A familiar face swam before my eyes, and I realized that the guy with the frizzy white hair had knelt beside me. "Iz," he asked anxiously, "are you okay?"

"What happened?" I asked.

"Maybe you'd better not try to stand up," someone said. "You could have a concussion."

No, I thought. *I don't have a concussion. I only made up that story to cover my mistakes.* I struggled to my feet even though I could feel nausea welling up in my throat. I was glad to let my weight rest against the white-haired boy.

The crowd of kids around me parted, and Mr. Crumpler pushed his way through. Everyone seemed to be trying to talk to him at once. "What's this about a hex sign?" he demanded.

I rubbed my face with my sleeve and saw raspberry smears. I recognized the greasy stains of lipstick, the same stuff I had spent the preceding night cleaning off my bathroom mirror. With so many kids gathered around me and staring, I was beginning to feel as if I were on exhibit. My mouth hurt, and I realized I must have split my lip when I fell.

"You'd better go to the hospital for X rays," said Mr. Crumpler. "These falls can be serious."

"I didn't fall," I protested. "Somebody hit me. Just leave me alone." All I wanted was to creep away someplace and take an aspirin. "I want to go wash my face," I added.

"I'll go with her," said a voice I recognized as Kaki's. She put her arm around me.

"I'm not going to faint," I assured her.

But when we got to the bathroom, I leaned heavily against the sink, shocked by the glimpse of myself in the cracked mirror. A greasy smear of red was on my forehead, and though I had obscured it by scrubbing at it with my sleeve, the original mark showed in a dye that had stained my skin. Someone had drawn a triangle on my forehead.

"Did you see who did it?" asked Kaki, sounding frightened.

I squirted slimy washroom soap in my palm and rubbed it on my face. "No. Whoever hit me came from behind." The water in both faucets was cold. I pulled handfuls of brown paper towels out of the dispenser, soaked them in soap, and scrubbed hard at my face. When I glanced in the mirror, most of the lipstick was gone, but my face was so pink I looked as if I had been boiled.

"You can hardly see the lipstick now," said Kaki reassuringly.

She was wrong. I could still make out traces of raspberry tint on my skin. "I'm going to sign out and go home," I said.

"You probably ought to go to the hospital and get checked out first, Iz, and I don't think you'd better drive yourself."

A mousy-looking woman I recognized as one of the school secretaries poked her head in the restroom door. "Isabel, Mr. Crumpler told me what happened. You poor thing. Can you walk?"

"I'm fine," I insisted. "But I'm going home."

The secretary's blue eyes bulged with alarm.

"Of course you want to go home, dear. But we'll have to get someone to drive you. You understand that when you're up to it, we'll need to fill out a report." Her lips pursed briefly. "We'll be notifying the police, of course."

"I'll drive her home, Mrs. Blandish," said Kaki.

"Good idea. Don't worry about signing out. I'll take care of that. Do you need help getting to the car?"

I found myself thinking that neither Kaki nor Mrs. Blandish were very much protection. I would have preferred my escorts to be armed. Whoever had attacked me was still out there somewhere.

Mrs. Blandish bustled off and left Kaki to walk me to the parking lot. I felt horrible.

"I'm parked way out by the power station," Kaki explained as we reached the lot. Belatedly I realized that she was carrying my backpack. I hadn't given it a thought. "You better sit here on the curb," she said, "and I'll go get it. That way you won't have to walk so far."

"It's okay." I glanced down the first row of cars to see my gleaming Corvette. "I'm parked close by. See?"

"But Iz," Kaki protested, "I can't drive the Corvette. Isn't it a stick shift?"

I smiled. "I don't need you to drive me."

"You're crazy," she said stoutly. "If you pass out behind the wheel and get killed, I'll never forgive myself."

"I'll be okay." I could feel anger rising in me when I thought of the person who was dogging my steps, stealing my computer, banging me on the head, smearing my face with greasy lipstick. I wanted to strike back somehow. But how? I didn't even know for certain who my enemy was.

"Rob!" Kaki screeched suddenly. "Would you talk to her? She wants to drive."

I lifted my aching head and saw Rob running toward us. I couldn't stop myself from smiling idiotically as he skidded to a stop at my side.

"Somebody knocked me out," I explained.

"I know." He exhaled. "The story's all over school. The hex sign and everything. I went to calculus but then I thought, this is stupid. It's not as if I can concentrate on calculus, and nobody's even going to notice that I'm gone." He took my hand. "How do you feel?" His eyes were shadowed with anxiety.

"Awful." I gently touched the top of my head.

"She wants to drive," Kaki repeated.

"It's okay, Kaki." said Rob. "I'll take her home."

Kaki threw up her hands. "Great! Be my guest."

My hand trembled as I handed Rob the keys. "How are you going to get your own car home?" I asked as we climbed into the Corvette.

"I left Carl my keys," he said. "Don't worry about it."

I could feel that my lip was swelling and I self-consciously touched it.

We drove slowly along the row of motley cars with matching purple parking stickers: a pickup with a Confederate flag on the back window; an economy car, its back window crammed with cute stuffed animals; a car painted black, its bumper covered with ecological stickers; a station wagon. Which of these anonymous classmates had stalked me and struck me down in the hallway? Who hated me—or Isabel—that much?

Rob glanced at me. "I wish I could wring Sarah Trimmer's neck for her," he said grimly. "She came running up to me in the hall, screaming that you were dead."

"D-dead?" My voice faltered.

"The girl's lucky I didn't have a heart attack right on the spot. Then she'd have had the body she wanted. You'd think she'd at least wait around long enough to get her story straight, the little twit." He was pale. "It was a good thing that the guy running up right behind her had better information." He glanced at me briefly. "Could you tell anything about what happened, Iz?"

I started to shake my head and then thought better of it. "I heard the bell ring, and then suddenly there was this crowd around me." I shivered. "I wonder what would have happened if the bell hadn't gone off. It must have scared away the attacker."

Rob's fingers tightened convulsively on the steeling wheel. "What were you doing outside anyway? You should have been in homeroom."

I explained about going into the office to tell Mr. Crumpler what had gone on at the gazebo the night before. "I wonder if it was Amy Rose who hit me." I rubbed the back of my head gingerly. "When she saw me going to the office, maybe she was afraid I was going to get her into trouble."

He frowned. "I talked to Amy Rose this morning."

"Already?" I looked at him, startled. I knew he had said he was going to confront her, but I hadn't expected it to be so soon.

"Yeah, I caught up with her before school. She says she didn't come into your house last night, and she swears she didn't steal anything or write that message on the mirror."

"She told you she didn't have anything to do with the coven either," I retorted. "And that was a lie."

"She explained that. She says what she's doing isn't really witchcraft," Rob said. "It's more like cultural enrichment."

"Sure. I'll bet."

"Just nice clean pagan rituals out of some old books. Stuff about nature—earth, wind, fire. It's all harmless, she says." He glanced at me. "I believe her."

I stared out the window. Trees along the road were drooping, heavy with the rain, and the slick pavement reflected the gray of the sky. A truck passed us, showing a row of golden running lights. Why was Rob suddenly defending Amy Rose? "How do you explain me getting knocked out?" I demanded. "Are you saying I did this to myself?"

He shook his head. "I'll tell you the truth. When Amy Rose is talking I believe her. Then I get away from her and I think I must be the most gullible guy in the world."

"She could have killed me!"

"I know." His voice was almost inaudible.

"You keep sticking up for her."

Rob rested his hand on my knee, but I couldn't interpret his expression. "Come on, give me a break."

"I've had about all I can take," I said, my voice rising. "This is no game. Do you realize that? I could end up dead like those people in the gruesome newspaper stories. Ritual killing. Love triangle."

"I'm not trying to defend Amy Rose, but do we really think she's dumb enough to put a hex sign on your forehead? I mean, think of all the people who already know she does that pagan stuff. It'd be stupid for her to be so obvious."

"Some people will do anything to get attention."

He heaved a sigh. We drove for a while in painful silence. Finally Rob spoke. "What am I supposed to think? First, your house at the beach gets burglarized and you get knocked out. Then your house here in town gets broken into and somebody slashes your mattress. Next, the door is accidentally left unlocked, and somebody just happens to run upstairs and steal your computer." I saw a muscle throb at the side of his tightly clenched mouth.

"You forgot to mention the message on the computer."

"And I forgot to mention the message on the computer," he repeated evenly.

"You don't believe me!" I cried. "Would you like to feel the lump on top of my head? Or are you saying I hit myself?"

He shook his head.

"You believe Amy Rose, but you don't believe me," I said.

Rob glanced at me. "It's hard to explain, Iz, but when I was talking to Amy Rose, it was like looking through clear glass. I don't think she was holding anything back."

I clutched my fist to my mouth. "You think I'm lying. Why don't you go ahead and say it? Tell me you think I'm a liar."

"I'm not saying you're a liar, but you can't be telling me the whole truth. You can't be!" He looked troubled. "I always used to have the feeling that we were playing some sort of game, and you were the only one who got to see the cards. Since you got back from the beach, it hasn't been like that a bit. It's been good." The muscle beside his mouth twitched. "But now all of a sudden this is feeling to me like old times." Rob's eyes met mine. "What is it you're not telling me?"

CHAPTER 14

"If you want to break up with me and go back to Amy Rose, that's fine." My voice sounded as if it belonged to someone else.

"You know I don't want that." Rob tried to smile. "Hey, I thought you said you didn't want to fight with me anymore."

"I guess I was wrong." I folded my arms and stared straight ahead. "I am telling the truth, whether you believe me or not." Tears stung my eyes. "I guess it doesn't matter anyway. I'm not sure I'm going to be staying around here."

"What are you saying?" Rob asked quietly.

"I may go live with my mother." My head ached. I wondered why I had never noticed before how empty and meaningless life was, and how futile it was to struggle when nothing was of any interest. I saw that we had reached my father's house. Rob pulled the car into the driveway without saying a word.

"How are you going to get home?" I whispered.

"Carl should be here pretty soon." He got out and opened the door for me. When I stood up shakily, he put his arms around me. "Don't go away," he said. "Don't even talk about it. It makes me crazy. Why do you want to go live with your mother? You don't even know her. Just go visit her at Christmas or something."

"I don't want to go anywhere." I sniffled. "I want to stay here with you."

An explosion sounded. All at once my blood seem to drain to my feet and I felt my knees give way. Rob held me tight so that I didn't fall. "It's just the car backfiring," he said.

I turned around to see Rob's old car turning into the lane. "I thought it was a gun," I said weakly.

Rob planted a kiss on the top of my head. "Look, we're both feeling pretty shaky right now. Sara scared me so much by telling me that you were dead, maybe I'm not even making sense."

But I knew he *was* making sense. Something about me didn't add up, and he was finally beginning to realize it.

I made out Carl's tombstone-shaped face behind the steering wheel of Rob's car.

"My chauffeur." Rob bowed ironically.

Carl leaned out of the car and scowled at us. "Hurry up, man. Don't just stand there. I'm in a hurry. I didn't even sign out."

"You better go with Carl," I said, giving Rob a little push. Carl revved up the old car's engine. The engine coughed and wheezed.

"Will you quit stomping on the gas!" Rob shouted.

Carl stuck his head out the car window. "Are you guys going to take all day or what? I'm telling you, I'm going to get in trouble if I don't get back to school."

"Nobody told you to come without signing out," said Rob, but he moved toward the car.

"Give me a call tonight," I said.

Rob got in and the old car drove away in a cloud of exhaust.

I went into the house and lay down on the living-room couch. I vaguely recalled that people with head injuries weren't supposed to let themselves fall asleep, and I sat bolt upright. Maybe I had better go by the hospital after all and get X rays. Anything seemed better than being alone with nothing to think about but that Rob didn't believe me.

I went to the hospital emergency room and got X rays, which took hours. It was past four when the emergency room doctors announced my skull wasn't fractured and let me go, warning me to report back if I started seeing double. I felt vaguely silly, as if I had gone to a lot of trouble for nothing.

Returning to the house, I felt a faint tremor of apprehension and had to force myself to go in. I had only been home a few minutes when the doorbell's ring startled me. I pulled the door open.

Amy Rose spun around to face me. "Isn't it enough that you got Rob away from me?" she spat. "Are you trying to fix it so nobody in school will speak to me, too?"

I took an involuntary step backward. She stepped into the house uninvited and glanced around, peeking curiously through the open double doors to the living room. "It must be nice to be rich," she said. "I suppose you think you can get away with anything."

I collapsed on a step at the bottom of the stairs. It was evident she wasn't carrying a concealed weapon, and I was a good bit bigger than she was, so I wasn't exactly afraid, but I touched the knot on my skull gingerly. "You seem to think that it's you who got attacked," I pointed out. "I just want to remind you that it was me."

She snorted disdainfully. "Well, I didn't do it."

I grabbed the banister for balance and stood up, realizing again how tiny Amy Rose was. It was easy to overlook because she was such a forceful personality, but height could matter in a case of assault, and I *was* taller by a good six or eight inches. I tried to envision Amy knocking me out, but the picture just wouldn't come together. The knot was on top of my head. She would have had to hop high up in the air to have hit me there. "Do you want a cup of tea or something?" I asked. A bizarre thought had occurred to me—I would actually be glad to have her company.

"You think I came all the way out here to drink tea?" Amy Rose demanded.

"I'm not exactly clear on why you did come," I said.

"To keep you from spreading any more rumors about me."

"I haven't spread a single rumor," I assured her. "I left school right after I got up off the ground."

When I turned my back on her the muscles at the base of my neck tightened, but I continued into the living room and kept moving through the dining room to the kitchen. After a minute she followed me.

I dropped a tea bag in a cup of water and slid it into the microwave.

"You could tell everybody I didn't do it," said Amy Rose. "I didn't, you know."

I shrugged. How did I know?

"I didn't!" she shouted.

When I thought of the moment before the blow struck, I recalled a faint impression of something large bearing down on me. Maybe that was why I couldn't quite picture Amy Rose as my attacker, though there wasn't anything definite I could pin down.

"I wouldn't put it past you to have staged the whole thing," she said darkly, "just to get me in trouble. I never hurt you."

I stared at her in blank astonishment. "What about putting Rob's ring in that nest of thorns and wrapping it up like a present?"

"Okay, I did that," she admitted. "I wanted to shake you up a little because I was jealous. I admit it. But it's not like a rose is a dangerous weapon or anything. That was kind of a joke."

I remembered the panic her "present" had stirred in me and found it hard to take a light-hearted view of the joke. The microwave pinged and I took out my mug.

"I guess I'll have some tea after all," said Amy Rose.

I pushed the mug across the table toward her and put in another for myself.

"It's not so easy to come into a new school in tenth grade," she said.

"I know."

"How would you know?" she said bitterly. "You've been sitting here, queen of the ant heap since you were born."

"My sister has moved around, though," I said.

"When you move into a new town, you have to make a place for yourself. Nobody does you any favors."

"I know," I said. "It's like you're invisible."

She looked at me in amazement. "You know, you're not a bit like I thought you'd be."

I reached for a packet of sweetener to have an excuse to turn my back on her and hide my confusion. "Really? Why do you say that?"

"You used to be so nice to me in this slimy, sneaky way."

"Why, thank you," I murmured, dumping white powder in the pallid liquid. What I needed was caffeine, I thought. Lots of caffeine. I dropped several more tea bags in the mug and put it back in the microwave.

Amy Rose stared. "Do you always use three tea bags?"

"Only when I've had a hard day."

A smile tugged at her lips. "You just seem like a completely different person."

"Don't you think people have a way of turning out to be different once you get to know them?"

"Nope. Not usually. Mostly with people, it's truth in advertising." She flushed. "Except for me, I guess. I had to go overboard to make an impression in this town."

"It worked," I observed.

"Not quite." She rested her chin on her cupped hand and looked depressed. "Having a reputation as a lunatic isn't what I had in mind."

I remembered the ceremony I had seen in the gazebo. Nature. Music. Dancing. Judging from what I had seen, Amy Rose could be telling the truth. Looking back now, the rituals seemed essentially harmless. Now I knew why Rob was convinced that she was telling the truth. Amy Rose wasn't the type to resort to brute force. She would be more likely to get her way by using her brains and imagination. But if she hadn't written on my mirror and stolen Isabel's diary, then who had?

"Well, for what it's worth, I don't really think that you're the one who attacked me." I took a sip of tea and promptly burned my mouth.

"I guess that's something." Amy Rose's gaze flicked to my face. "So you'll tell everybody at school that I didn't hit you?"

"Sure."

A sudden smile changed her face, and with a sharp squeeze of the heart I saw why Rob had been attracted to her. Probably he would go back to her when he learned the truth about me.

"It probably won't do any good," she said. "But I do appreciate your offer." She stood up. "I guess it doesn't matter that much, anyway," she added. "It looks like my father's about to get transferred again."

"I'm sorry about that," I said.

She shrugged. "It's ruining my life, that's all."

I walked with her to the front door, then watched as she strode to her car, a small, determined figure in the deepening dusk. When I shut the door it occurred to me that I ought to check on my father. I was a little surprised that he hadn't shown himself all afternoon.

He didn't answer when I knocked. I pushed his door open and found him lying on the bed, gasping. Blue veins stood out at his temples, and his thin hands clutched at the sheet.

"I'm going to call the doctor," I said, reaching for the phone by the bed.

His eyes were wide with fear as I dialed the emergency number. I gave the dispatcher careful directions to the house, then I sat on the edge of my father's bed and took his cool hand in mine. My heart fluttered under my breastbone. "They won't be long," I said, hoping that I was right. "They'll have oxygen in the ambulance and everything you need." I tried to make my voice calm. *I should have checked on him sooner,* I told myself.

I leaped up and went to rummage in his medicine cabinet, but nothing was helpfully labeled "for the heart" or "to help with breathing." Every container had names I didn't recognize.

It seemed an eternity until a banging on the door announced the arrival of the paramedics. I ran to let them in and then stood back out of their way. Minutes later they rolled my father to the front door on a stretcher. He was already hooked up to equipment, and transparent tubes ran into his nostrils. "Liz!" he gasped.

I ran to him. "I'm sorry," he gasped. "Be . . . careful."

The hair at the nape of my neck lifted gently. He was warning me. But of what?

"Stand back," one of the men said. They rolled the stretcher out to the ambulance and slid it into the back of the truck.

"Is he going to be all right?" I cried, as the doors slammed shut.

"He's in good hands," said the young medic, running around to jump in beside the driver.

I watched as the emergency vehicle careened down the lane, its red light whirling in the dusk. Its siren rent the silence, and the woods gave back an echo. I wondered if I should have gotten in the ambulance with him.

My father's warning rang in my ears. As I turned to go upstairs, it seemed as if the house were holding its breath. Silence pressed against my eardrums.

The phone rang and I snatched it up.

"Hi," Rob's voice came out of the receiver. "How're you doing?"

"Not so good," I said hoarsely.

"What's wrong?"

"The paramedics just rushed Dad to the hospital," I said. "I wish I had checked on him sooner."

"You mean you're at the house by yourself now?" Rob asked sharply.

"Yes." I glanced around me. The emptiness of the house seemed ominous now. The window looked out on thick woods where darkness was gathering. A faint high whistle, almost a rattle, sounded in the silence. "What's that?" I whispered.

"Iz?" Rob asked. "Are you all right?"

"It must have been the wind in the fireplace," I said weakly. I wished I had thought to turn on all the lights downstairs before I had came up to my room.

"I'm coming," Rob said.

"No!" I cried. "I don't want to stay here! I'm too scared. Meet me somewhere."

"Chico's?" suggested Rob. "Do you know the Mexican restaurant near the old water plant?"

"I think so. I'm on my way." When I hung up, my heart was pounding so hard I felt dizzy.

CHAPTER 15

Rob was waiting for me when I got to Chico's. It was dark in the restaurant, and I couldn't read his expression. Brightly colored piñatas hung from the ceiling, along with an oversized parrot on a swing, surreal shapes in the darkness. I wished Rob had chosen a more cheerfully lit place.

Rows of glasses glistened behind a deserted long bar. We groped our way to a booth. Sliding into its high banquette seat was like climbing into a cave of black cushions. I could feel Rob's warm breath ruffling my hair as he slid his arm around me. "I'm sorry about your father," he murmured. "What do the doctors say?"

"I haven't called the hospital yet." I sneaked a sideways look at him. "The last thing he said to me as they rolled him into the ambulance was 'I'm sorry. Be careful.' It spooked me. It's as if he knew something I don't know."

"Like what?"

I shook my head. "I don't know. But he seemed to be *warning* me."

"Maybe you'd better not go back to the house tonight."

"Maybe he was only apologizing for being a rotten father. He has a lot to apologize for." I unfolded my napkin in my lap. "I talked to Amy Rose this afternoon. I think you're right. She's telling the truth."

"So who attacked you and stole the computer?"

"I'm not sure." I glanced at him. "I guess that's why I'm afraid to be in the house by myself now."

"Hey, hey, hey," said Rob, softly, putting his fingers under my chin to lift my face.

I pressed my lips to his hungrily, as if I knew this was to be our last kiss. The shadows around us seemed to be closing in.

Rob drew away from me and suddenly traced the curl at my temple with his finger. "You aren't Isabel, are you?" I scarcely recognized his voice.

"Of course I am." I stared at him wide-eyed.

He shook his head. "No, I never felt this way

about Isabel. Never."

I reached for his hand but he shook me off. The whites of his eyes gleamed in the dim light. He was staring at me as if he had never seen me before. "All that stuff you couldn't remember. Like my middle name. You couldn't remember my middle name because you never knew it, did you? And that little curl of yours is in the wrong place!"

I felt sick. I was losing him, and I couldn't bear it.

"Where's Iz?" he whispered. "What have you done with her?" His eyes grew round. "You're her twin, aren't you? Did you kill her? Did you murder her so you could take her place?"

"No!" I cried.

"Why did you let me think you were her?" he demanded.

All my reasons came flooding back to me. It struck me suddenly how hopelessly inadequate they were.

Rob grabbed my arms and held me so tightly that it hurt. "You are telling me the truth now, aren't you?"

"You're hurting me!" I cried.

He let go. "I can't believe this," he said. "This can't be happening."

I clenched and unclenched my fists under the table. "I can show you my passport if you want proof of who I am."

"None of this makes sense to me," he said miserably. "It's crazy."

I was suddenly morbidly self-conscious. I knew I couldn't explain that he himself had been part of the reason I had been drawn into the strange game of impersonating my sister.

"I suppose when they notified me of Isabel's death it was a shock," I said finally. "I couldn't quite face it. I think maybe I had the crazy idea that I could get close to her by taking her place." I shook my head sadly. "It didn't work out that way, though."

He swore under his breath.

A waitress appeared. "Sorry, I didn't see you guys come in," she said, taking out her pencil. "What will you have?"

Rob stared at her blankly.

"We need more time to decide," I said. "A *lot* more time."

"Sure, honey," said the waitress hastily. "Take as much time as you need." I heard her footsteps on the tile floor as she beat a retreat.

"You have an answer for everybody, don't you?" Rob said bitterly. "You're real cool. Look at the way you carried this off—going to class, wearing Isabel's clothes." He stared. "What am I supposed to call you now?"

"Liz," I said. "Elizabeth is my name. Liz for short."

"Iz's twin," he said numbly. "Why should I believe Isabel's dead? Why should I believe anything you say when all you've done is lie to me?"

Rob slid out of the booth and stood a minute beside the table, staring at me. I saw his stunned face through my tears. And then suddenly he was gone.

I felt too heavy to move. I sat there for several minutes, waiting for the shock that had hit my body to sink into my numbed brain. The sound of low voices registered, and so did the chink of bottles and glasses. Business must be picking up at the bar. Blindly I groped for my purse, and somehow managed to stumble out of the restaurant.

When I stepped out into the cool night, I had the oddest sense of being set adrift. It was as if the law of gravity had snapped and I had been let loose to float in the featureless black of outer space with no way to get home. I hugged myself and shivered. Only a few bright stars shone through the city's haze.

The thought crossed my mind that perhaps I

should go to the hospital and check on my father's condition. But I knew that I didn't really care about him. He had never been a father to me.

Climbing into the Corvette, I told myself, *this is not my life. I can walk away any time.* But I knew it was a lie. Isabel's life had become my life. And if I left now, I would be walking away from what I cared about most in the world. Rob's face swam before my eyes. It was over. No wonder he hated me—I had lied to him from the beginning. I felt sick with self-loathing.

Sometime tonight a flight would leave for Rome. Or London. I was in a state of half-consciousness that seemed familiar. I realized it was like the way I felt when I woke up in a hotel room, foggily unsure of what country I was in and not even sure which way the bathroom was. I decided to pack my bag and drive at once to the airport.

I have no recollection whatever of driving back to my father's house. Light beamed out its windows, casting misshapen shadows on the driveway. I felt a sick clutch of anxiety and would have turned the car around and left immediately, if I hadn't needed to get my passport.

The door of the car slammed with a solid finality when I got out, and my shoes scraped on the pavement as I walked to the front door. I took a deep breath as I slid the key in the lock. I assured myself that I would be out of the house in minutes, yet the muscles at the back of my neck tightened as I stepped in.

I ran upstairs. When I stepped into the bedroom, my stomach squeezed suddenly and I froze. Something looked different. Isabel's fuzzy sweater should have been hanging over the back of the chair. I closed my eyes and visualized the way the room had looked when Rob and I had rushed in the night before. I was almost certain the sweater had been on the chair when I left that night, but it wasn't there now.

With my heart pounding, I went over to the closet and slid its doors open. Glancing at the stuffed animals on the top shelf, I saw that Mr. Jeremy Fisher was missing. He was the stuffed animal I usually noticed first because he had long spindly legs that dangled off the edge of the closet shelf. Abruptly I began tossing the stuffed animals down. Jeremy Fisher wasn't the only animal missing. I remembered a white unicorn, a large dragon, and a battered teddy bear with a missing eye. All three had been too large to stick in a pocket or a backpack.

I hadn't noticed the stuffed animals when I was dressing that morning, I realized, so I couldn't swear whether the missing ones had been there then or not. But didn't it make sense that they had vanished at the same time as the sweater?

My throat had gone dry. I stuffed my passport in my purse, hoisted the half-filled suitcase, and ran downstairs.

The silence of the house was eerie. I hesitated on the landing. I saw that the front door was ajar and a chill ran up my spine.

The door flew open and Rob was there, the porch light shining on his dark hair. "Are you all right?" he cried.

I ran downstairs, dropped the suitcase, and flung my arms around him, sobbing.

He clutched me tightly. "When I saw the door was open I was scared. I didn't know what might be going on."

I dashed tears out of my eyes. "Rob, Isabel is alive!"

"What are you telling me?" He pulled away and stared at me.

"She's alive! Her favorite sweater and her favorite stuffed animals are missing from her room! Nobody else would have taken those things but Isabel! It must have been Isabel that wrote 'Stay away from Rob' on the bathroom mirror and sent the message 'Find my killer' to the computer."

"None of what you're saying makes any sense," he said unsteadily. "Do you realize that? If Isabel's alive, why on earth would she write 'Find my killer'?"

"Because she was *pretending* to be dead!" I took a deep breath. "The police found a girl's body at the beach house, but a shotgun blast had made the face unrecognizable. What if the police were wrong about it being Isabel? What if the body belonged to somebody else?"

"Who?" he cried. "And if Iz isn't dead, why would she pretend that she was?"

"Because she was afraid?" I hazarded. "If another girl answered the door that night, and the light was behind her, the murderer would only have seen a silhouette. It probably never crossed his mind that somebody else would come to the door at Isabel's beach house."

"But who was this mysterious victim?"

"I don't know," I said helplessly. "Only Isabel can tell us that. But suppose Isabel knows that the person's murder was a mistake. Suppose she knows that she was the killer's real target and that's why she went into hiding. She let me fill in for her, hoping that the murderer would go after me instead of her."

"I don't believe it," said Rob. "Iz wouldn't do that."

"I guess I was expendable." I remembered my father's last minute warning as he was being taken to the hospital. But it was too little warning and too late. It was plain which of his daughters mattered most. "If Isabel's alive, Dad must have known it," I went on doggedly. "She must have been hiding in his room when she sent that message to my computer upstairs. I could hear her laughing. I guess she thought it was a good joke."

Rob frowned. "Maybe she can explain."

"It's Isabel that you love, isn't it?" I took a stumbling step back, unable to look at him. "It's always been Isabel you wanted." I choked. "I guess I'd better go."

Rob reached for me and held me tightly. "She's not the one I love. You know better than that."

I buried my face against his shirt, trying to untangle my few rational thoughts from my wildly surging emotions.

"I've been driving around town like a crazy person trying to figure all this stuff out," said Rob. "Jeez, the shock! I was staggered. Here you were telling me that Iz was dead and that you weren't who I thought you were. After that I wasn't even listening to what you had to say. I guess I acted like a jerk."

I shook my head. "No, it was all my fault."

"Listen, if Iz is alive, we'll track her down and make her explain. The two of us can deal with this."

"Okay." I smiled mistily at him. "Somehow we'll find Isabel and make everything right."

But how? How could we possibly find my clever and devious twin if she was determined to stay out of sight? And why hadn't she warned me that I was in danger? An aching loss weighed my heart when I admitted to myself that the perfect sister I had longed for had never existed.

Now I was trapped. Staying here, my life was at risk, but I couldn't leave town—I couldn't leave Rob.

Rob touched my lips gently with his finger and bent his head to kiss me. We would find Isabel, I told myself desperately. We *had* to. It looked as if my life depended on it.